Great Figures in History

Mother Teresa

Agnes Gonxha Bojaxhiu

Y. kids
www.myykids.com

Great Figures in History

Mother Teresa

Copyright © 2008 YoungJin Singapore Pte. Ltd.
World rights reserved. No part of this publication may be stored in a retrieval system, transmitted, or reproduced in any way, including but not limited to photocopies, photographs, magnetic data, or other records, without the prior agreement and written permission of the publisher.

ISBN: 978-981-057552-6
Printed and bound in the Republic of Korea.

How to contact us
E-mail: feedback@myykids.com

Credits
Adaptation & Art: SAM (Special Academic Manga)
Production Manager: Suzie Lee
Editorial Services: Publication Services, Inc.
Developmental Editor: Rachel Lake, Publication Services, Inc.
Editorial Manager: Lorie Donovan, Publication Services, Inc.
Book Designer: SAM (Special Academic Manga)
Cover Designer: Litmus
Production Control: Misook Kim, Sangjun Nam

With the participation of

mda
Media Development Authority
Singapore

A Message To Readers

Welcome to the *Great Figures in History* series by **Y. kids**. These biographies of some of the world's most influential people will take you on an exciting journey through history. These are the stories of great scientists, leaders, artists, and inventors who have shaped the world we live in today.

How did these people make a difference in their world? You will see from their stories that things did not always come easily for them. Just like many of us, they often had problems in school or at home. Some of them had to overcome poverty and hardship. Still others faced discrimination because of their religion, their gender, or the color of their skin. But all of these *Great Figures in History* worked tirelessly and succeeded despite many challenges.

Sing, an adventurer from Planet Mud, will be your guide through the lives of these famous historical figures. The people of Sing's planet are in great danger, facing a strange disease that drains their mental powers. To save the people of Planet Mud, Sing must travel through space and time and try to capture the mental powers of several *Great Figures in History*. Will Sing be successful in his journey? You will have to read to find out!

If you enjoy this story, visit our website, **www.myykids.com**, to see other books in the *Great Figures in History* series. You can also visit the website to let us know what you liked or didn't like about the book, or to leave suggestions for other stories you would like to see.

A Note To Parents and Teachers

Y. kids welcomes you to Educational Manga Comics. We certainly hope that your child or student will enjoy reading our books. The Educational Manga Comics present material in "manga" form, a comic story style developed in Japan that is enjoying enormous popularity with young people today. These books deliver substantive educational content in a fun and easy-to-follow visual format.

At the end of each book, you will find bonus features—including a historical timeline, a summary of the individual's enduring cultural significance, and a list of suggested Web and print resources for related information—to enhance your reader's learning experience. Our website, **www.myykids.com**, offers supplemental activities, resources, and study material to help you incorporate **Y. kids** books into your child's reading at home or in the a classroom curriculum.

Our entire selection of Educational Manga Comics, covering math, science, history, biographies, and literature, is available on our website. The website also has a feedback option, and we welcome your input.

CONTENTS

WHO'S WHO?

Young Teresa

MOTHER TERESA

Born Agnes Gonxha Bojaxhiu, baptismal name 'Agnes,' in Yugoslavia, she became a nun when she was 18 years old. She moved to India and spent her life helping the poor and sick. She won the Nobel Peace Prize for her achievements.

DRANE BOJAXHIU

She is the mother of 'Mother Teresa'. As a devout Catholic, she played a big role in instilling religious faith in Mother Teresa.

FATHER VAN EXEM

As the head of the Sisters of Loreto in Calcutta, India, he was a source of strength for Mother Teresa when she was distressed by poverty in India.

SUBASHINI DAS

Subashini Das was a student of Mother Teresa when she was appointed to teach at St. Mary's High School. She was the first to volunteer for Mother Teresa's work to help the poor. She was always at Mother Teresa's side and did much charity work.

NUNS OF THE MISSIONARIES OF CHARITY

Nuns that worked for the Missionaries of Charity. They are nuns who were touched by Mother Teresa's cause and joined her order.

The residents of Planet Mud in the Andromeda Galaxy have been suffering from a strange illness.

The Planet Mud Disease Control Committee has reported that this plague was caused by a so-called Confusion Virus that drains mental energy from people. Once affected by the virus, people suffer strange symptoms such as tiredness and frustration.

The Planet Mud Disease Control Committee has suggested a solution to this plague. They hope to clone aspects of the mental energy from some of the greatest souls of Planet Earth. When the Cam-cam records the lives of the great souls, it can collect copies of their unique and special mental energy. This mental energy is then refined into crystallized mental energy to be injected into the suffering residents of Planet Mud.

It is Sing's job to distill the crystallized fairy of each great soul's mental energy.

Sing An explorer from Planet Mud. He was dispatched by the Planet Mud Disease Control Committee to collect mental energies from the great souls of Planet Earth.

Alpha Plus Sing's assistant robot, who keeps him out of trouble. His vast store of information can solve many questions during their adventures.

Cam-cam An invention from Planet Mud. When it records the lives of the great people, their mental energy is copied and refined.

Compassion Fairy When dusted with the powder from this fairy, a person will recognize that it is more rewarding to sacrifice personal own needs to meet the needs of others.

Grr.

Grr.

COME ON, CAN'T YOU WRITE IT FOR ME?

I AM TOO BUSY.

SNORT

BUT IT IS YOUR JOB TO WRITE OUR REPORTS!

YOU ARE MY ROBOT. I AM YOUR MASTER.

AREN'T YOU SUPPOSED TO LISTEN TO ME AND FOLLOW MY ORDERS?

WELL, SOMETIMES. BUT YOU'RE NOT THE GREATEST MASTER EITHER.

JUST LOOK AT ME.

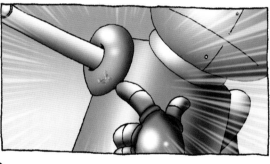

I RUST BECAUSE YOU GIVE ME ONLY CHEAP OIL. IF YOU REALLY CARED ABOUT ME, YOU WOULDN'T LET ME RUST!

You both need to respect and value each other.

9

You should follow the example of Mother Teresa.

**Mother Teresa,
or Teresa of Calcutta,
1910—1997**

Mother Teresa was born Agnes Gonxha Bojaxhiu in Yugoslavia. She became a nun and traveled to India, where she dedicated her life to helping the poor and sick. She received the Nobel Peace Prize in 1979 for her work.

IS OUR NEXT MISSION TO COLLECT THE SPIRITUAL ENERGY OF MOTHER TERESA?

Yes, that's right. You two will travel to Yugoslavia to fill the Cam-cam with the energy of Mother Teresa.

WAIT, I HAVE A QUESTION.

IF SOMEONE SHARED HER SPIRITUAL ENERGY, WOULD HE LOVE AND CARE ABOUT OTHERS AS SHE DID?

Yes, he would.

GREAT! I WILL USE HER SPIRITUAL ENERGY TO MAKE ALPHA PLUS WRITE MY REPORT.

AND I WILL USE HER SPIRITUAL ENERGY TO MAKE SING BUY BETTER OIL FOR ME.

HEH-HEH

LET'S GO SEE MOTHER TERESA!

11

EPISODE 1
GOOD AGNES

Skopje, Macedonia, 1915

AGNES! AGNES, WHERE ARE YOU?

LAZAR, HAVE YOU SEEN AGNES?

Age: eleven years old

I AM LOOKING FOR HER, TOO.

Lazar: eight years old

AGNES! AGNES!

AGNES!

AGNES!

AGNES, COME ON OUT!

YOU ARE A TROUBLEMAKER. WHERE ARE YOU?

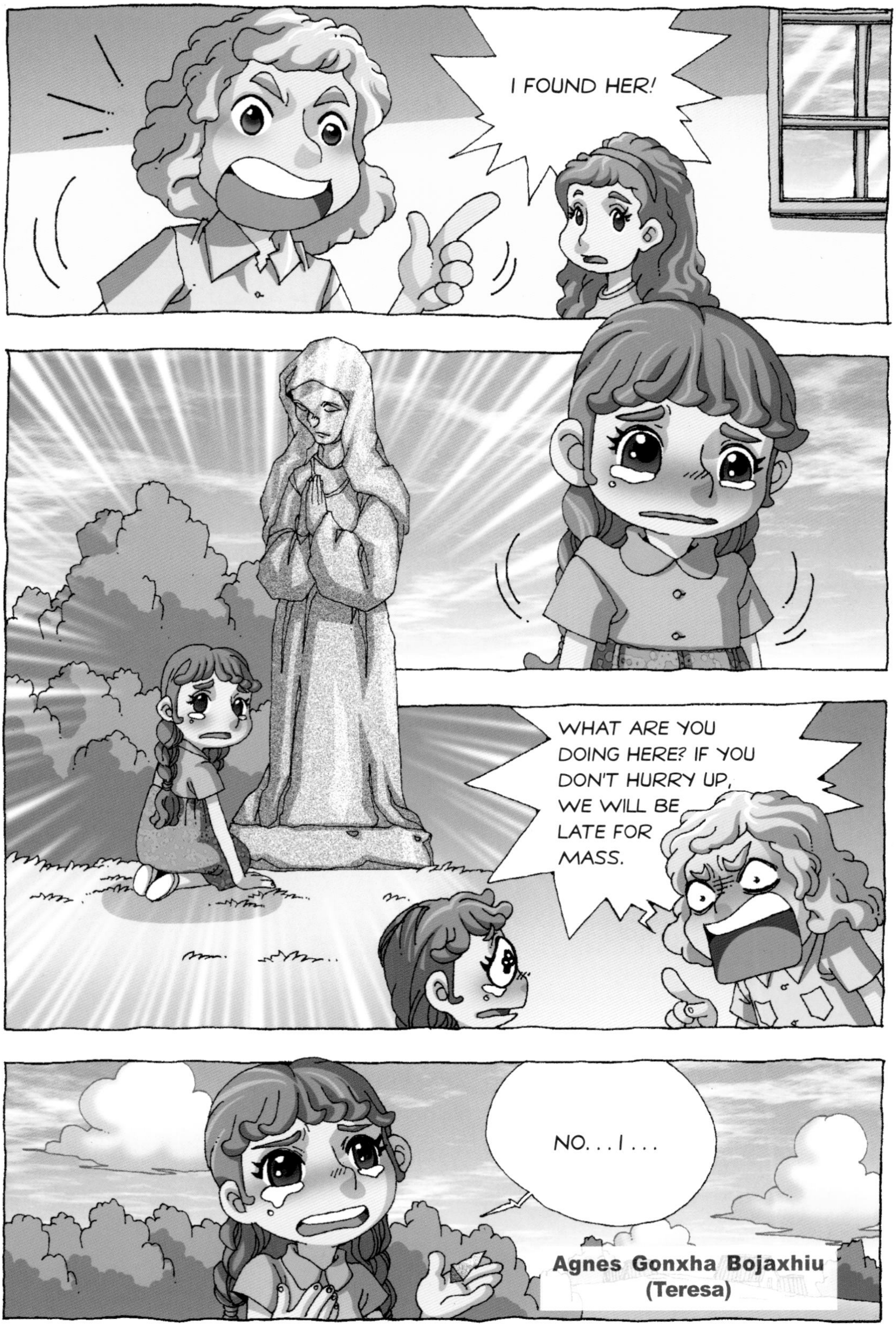
I FOUND HER!
WHAT ARE YOU DOING HERE? IF YOU DON'T HURRY UP, WE WILL BE LATE FOR MASS.
NO. . . I . . .
Agnes Gonxha Bojaxhiu (Teresa)

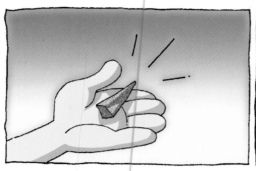

I BROKE THE NOSE OFF THE VIRGIN MARY'S STATUE!

BOO-HOO

ALL I WANTED TO DO WAS CATCH A BUTTERFLY...

UH-OH, LOOK WHAT YOU DID.

WHAT AM I GOING TO DO IF THE VIRGIN MARY DIES BECAUSE OF ME?

WHAT DO YOU MEAN?

PEOPLE DIE WHEN THEY CAN'T BREATHE.

THE VIRGIN MARY CAN'T BREATHE BECAUSE I BROKE HER NOSE . . . GOD WILL PUNISH ME!

HA, HA, HA.

BOO-HOO

THEN WE WILL BE IN BIG TROUBLE. LET ME HELP YOU.

MOTHER!

Drane Bojaxhiu Agnes's Mother

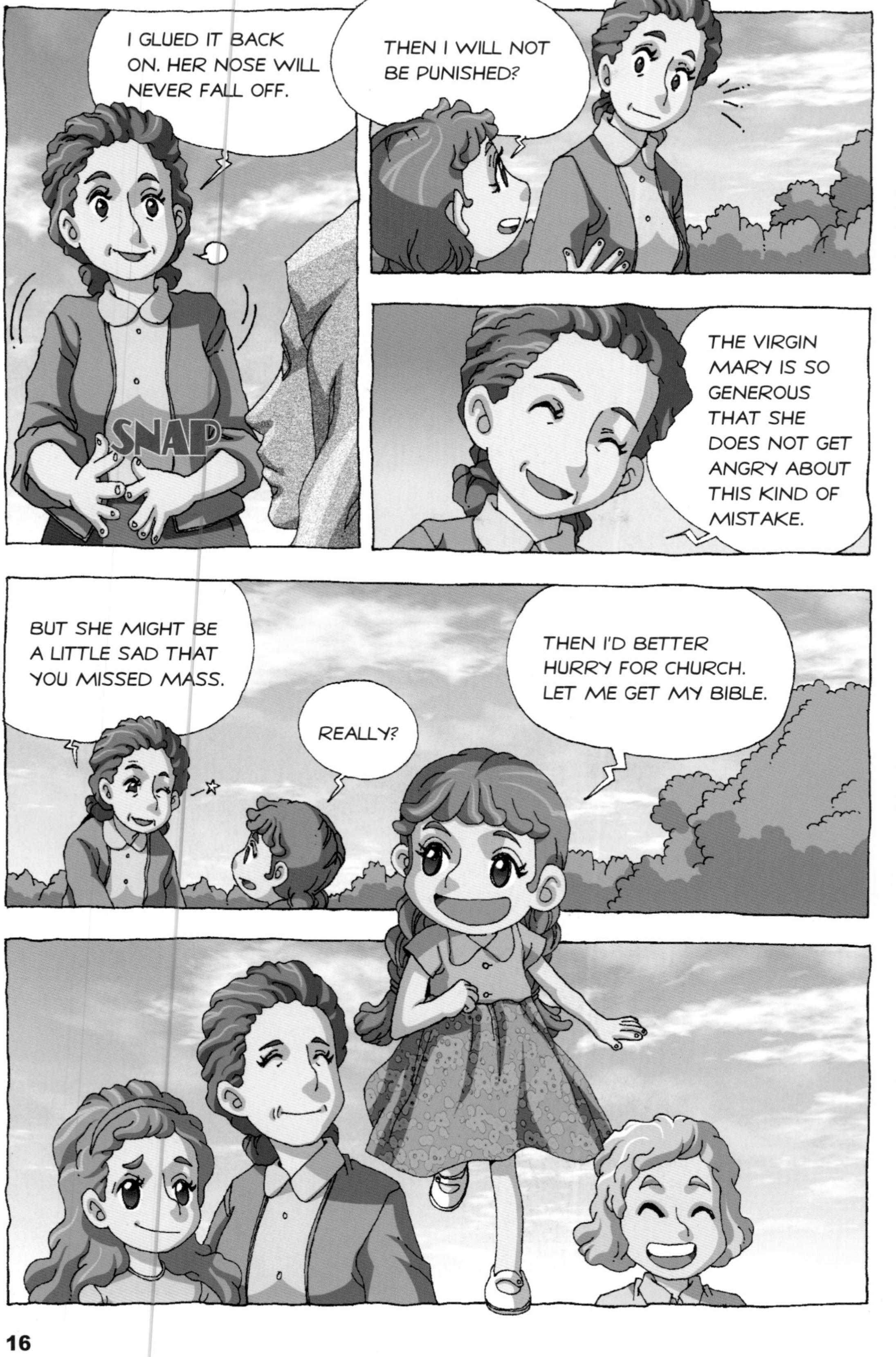

I GLUED IT BACK ON. HER NOSE WILL NEVER FALL OFF.
SNAP
THEN I WILL NOT BE PUNISHED?
THE VIRGIN MARY IS SO GENEROUS THAT SHE DOES NOT GET ANGRY ABOUT THIS KIND OF MISTAKE.
BUT SHE MIGHT BE A LITTLE SAD THAT YOU MISSED MASS.
REALLY?
THEN I'D BETTER HURRY FOR CHURCH. LET ME GET MY BIBLE.

Agnes was born on August 27, 1910, the youngest of three children of an Albanian family.

Her mother was a devoted Catholic who never missed the Mass.

Agnes was strongly influenced by her mother's faith in God.

Like a light guiding ships at night, Agnes's mother showed Agnes how to do the right thing.

WOW!

In particular, her mother taught her the joy of helping others.

I AM NOT GOING TO EAT THESE.

THESE APPLES TASTE SOUR.

YOU MUST EAT THEM, BECAUSE THEY ARE PRECIOUS FOODS THAT GOD GAVE US.

WELL, GOD SHOULD HAVE GIVEN US TASTIER APPLES.

THEY AREN'T SO SOUR. YOU ARE PICKY.

NO, I'M NOT. THEY ARE REALLY BAD.

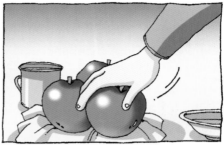

?

WHERE ARE YOU TAKING THOSE APPLES?

I WILL TAKE THESE APPLES TO SOMEONE WHO REALLY NEEDS THEM. DO YOU WANT TO JOIN ME?

WHO WOULD WANT TO EAT THOSE SOUR APPLES?

YOU WILL SEE IF YOU COME WITH ME.

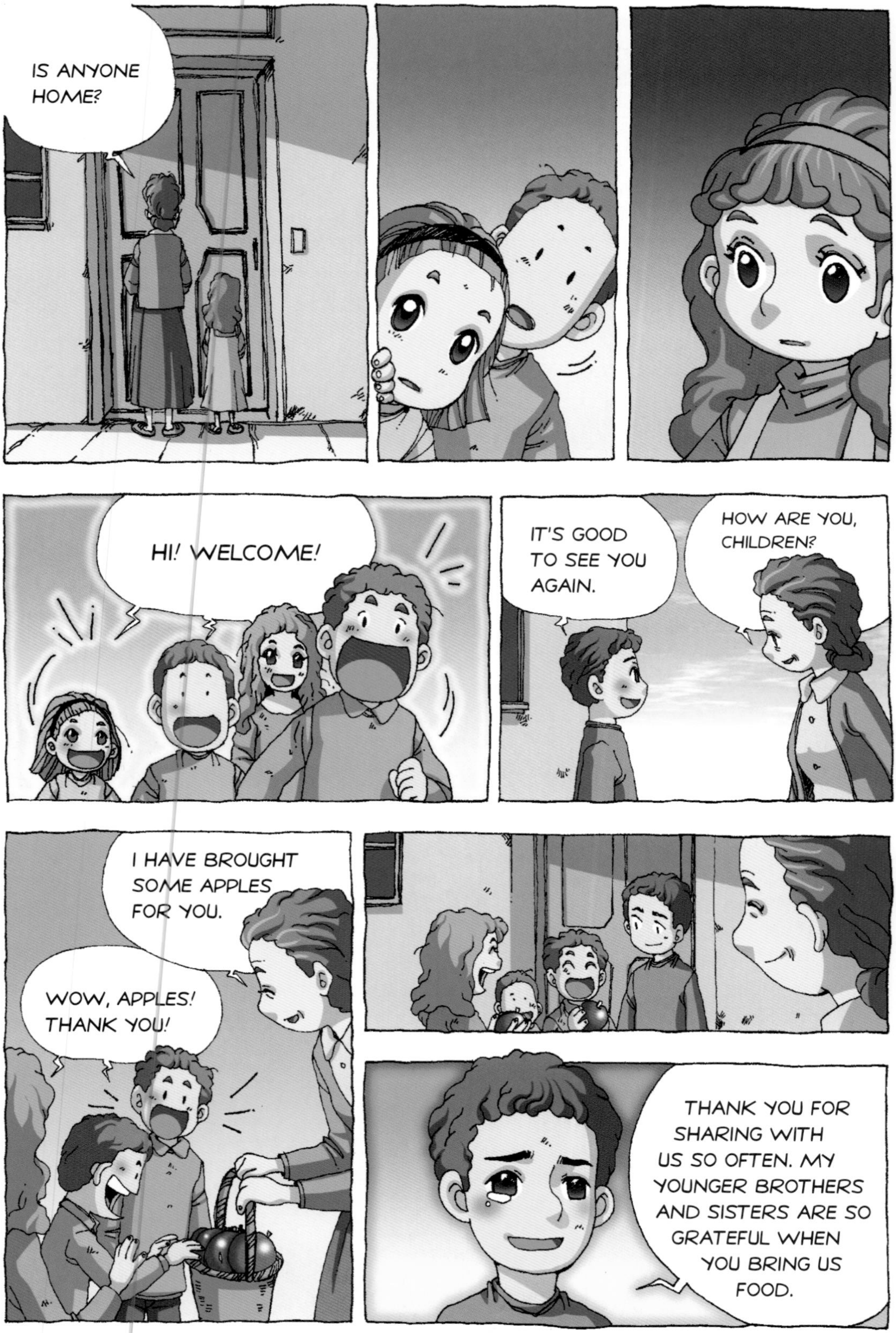
IS ANYONE HOME?
HI! WELCOME!
IT'S GOOD TO SEE YOU AGAIN.
HOW ARE YOU, CHILDREN?
I HAVE BROUGHT SOME APPLES FOR YOU.
WOW, APPLES! THANK YOU!
THANK YOU FOR SHARING WITH US SO OFTEN. MY YOUNGER BROTHERS AND SISTERS ARE SO GRATEFUL WHEN YOU BRING US FOOD.

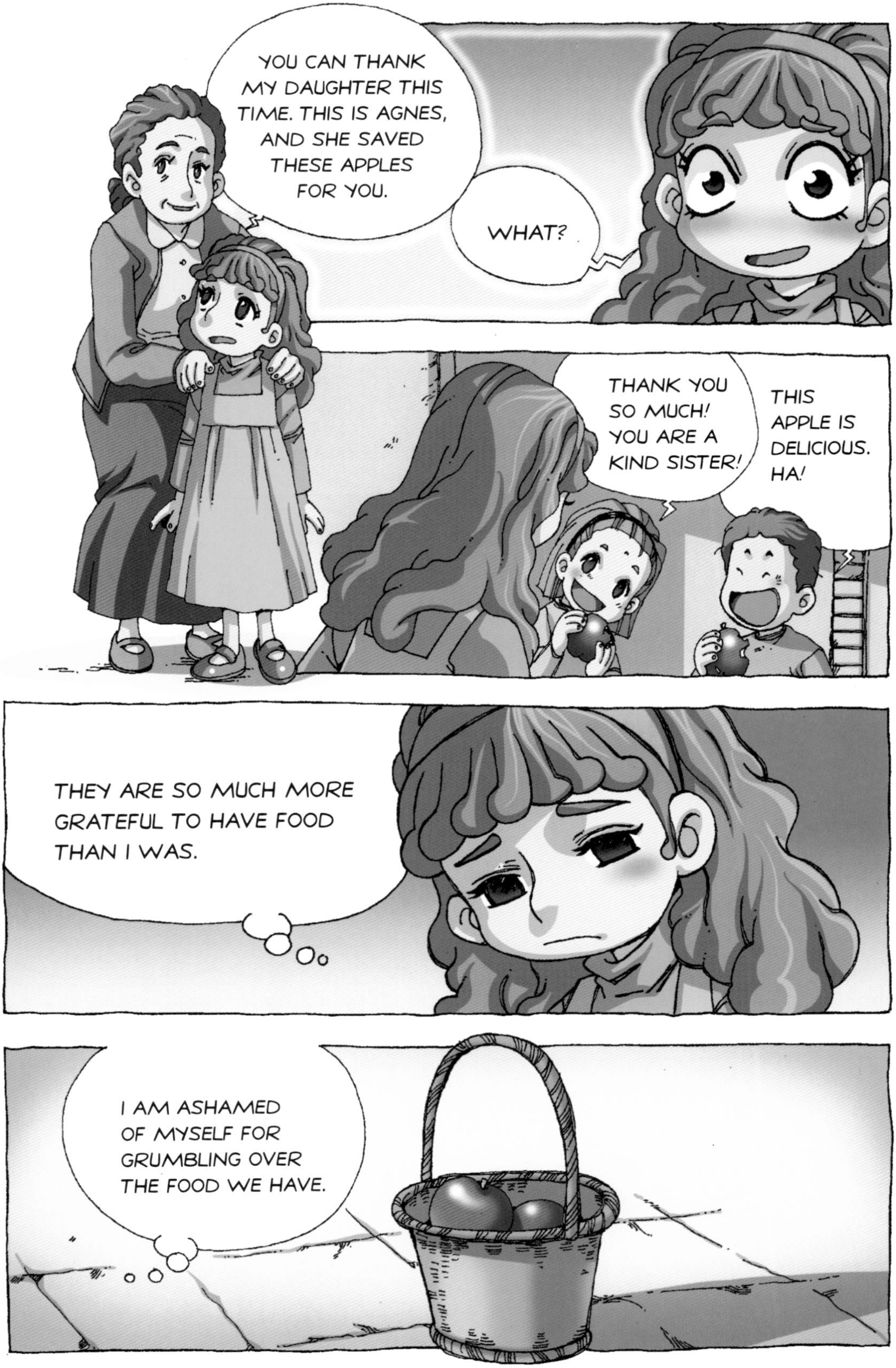
YOU CAN THANK MY DAUGHTER THIS TIME. THIS IS AGNES, AND SHE SAVED THESE APPLES FOR YOU.
WHAT?
THANK YOU SO MUCH! YOU ARE A KIND SISTER!
THIS APPLE IS DELICIOUS. HA!
THEY ARE SO MUCH MORE GRATEFUL TO HAVE FOOD THAN I WAS.
I AM ASHAMED OF MYSELF FOR GRUMBLING OVER THE FOOD WE HAVE.

COME HERE AND HAVE SOME APPLE. I DON'T WANT TO EAT WITHOUT SHARING WITH YOU.

WELL, THANK YOU.

HMM, IT TASTES VERY GOOD. WHAT HAPPENED?

DID YOU ENJOY YOUR APPLE?

STRANGELY, YES. IT WAS TOTALLY DIFFERENT FROM WHEN I ATE THEM AT HOME.

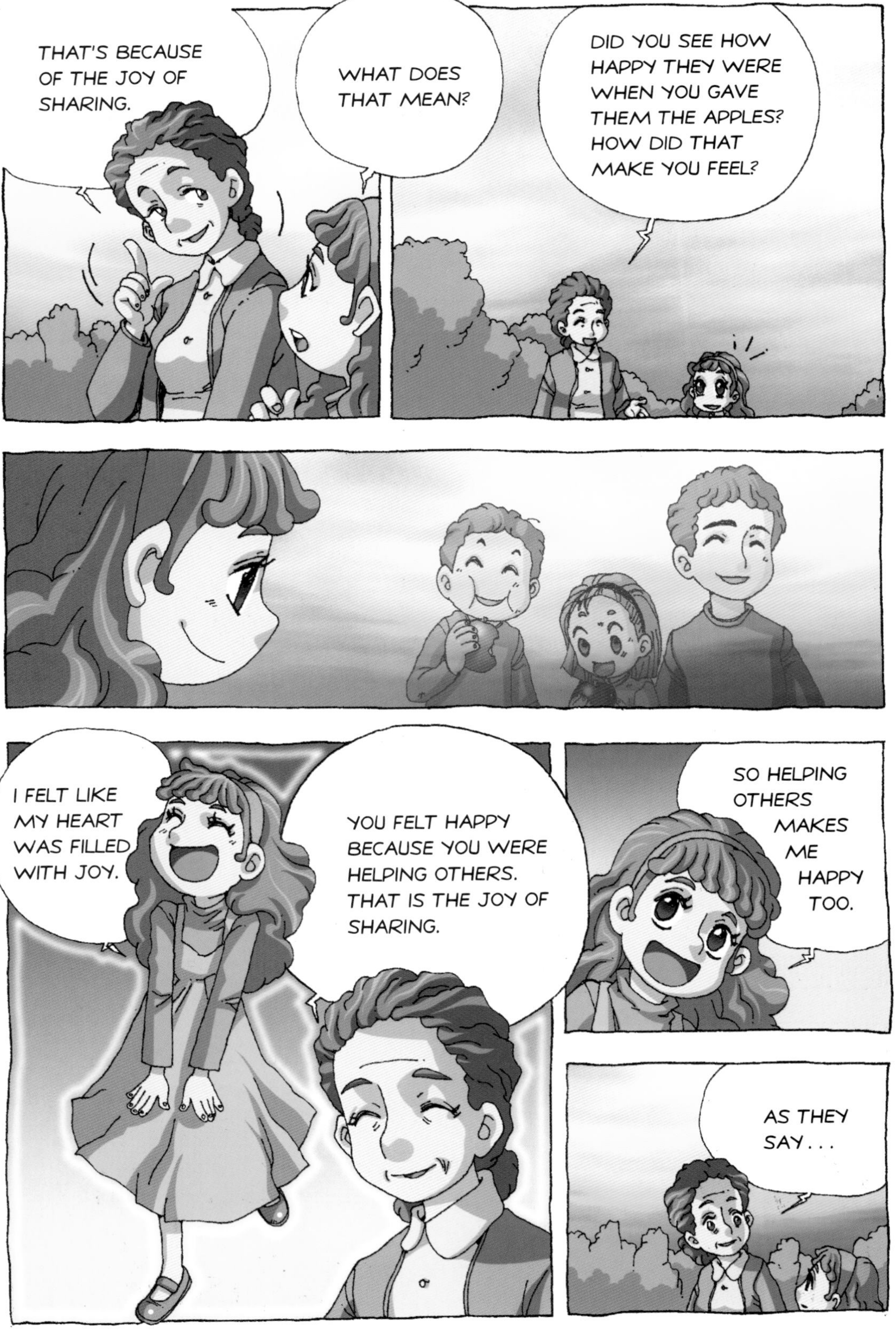
THAT'S BECAUSE OF THE JOY OF SHARING.
WHAT DOES THAT MEAN?
DID YOU SEE HOW HAPPY THEY WERE WHEN YOU GAVE THEM THE APPLES? HOW DID THAT MAKE YOU FEEL?
I FELT LIKE MY HEART WAS FILLED WITH JOY.
YOU FELT HAPPY BECAUSE YOU WERE HELPING OTHERS. THAT IS THE JOY OF SHARING.
SO HELPING OTHERS MAKES ME HAPPY TOO.
AS THEY SAY . . .

"A SORROW SHARED IS BUT HALF THE TROUBLE,

AND A JOY THAT'S SHARED IS A JOY MADE DOUBLE."

I SEE! FROM NOW ON, I WILL TRY TO HELP OTHERS AS MUCH AS I CAN!

GOOD, MY DARLING.

NOW I UNDERSTAND!

NOW I KNOW WHY AGNES BECAME A MISSIONARY. HER MOTHER MUST HAVE TOLD HER TO. AM I RIGHT?

THAT'S NONSENSE.

YOU UNDERSTAND WHAT?

HER MOTHER COULD NOT MAKE THAT KIND OF DECISION FOR AGNES.

MOST PEOPLE BECOME MISSIONARIES BECAUSE THEY HEAR GOD'S CALL.

GOD'S CALL? HOW CAN THEY HEAR THAT?

UMM...

AGNES MUST HAVE HAD A VERY GOOD REASON FOR CHOOSING HER LIFE'S WORK!

BANG

WE WILL HAVE TO CONTINUE WATCHING TO SEE HOW AGNES BECOMES A MISSIONARY.

EPISODE 2
A BIG DECISION

Montenegro

This was a sacred place for Catholics to go to pray.

Young Agnes, a devoted Catholic, came here often to offer prayers of thanksgiving to God.

Agnes joined a youth group at her church. They studied and prayed together.

Father Jambrenkovic, the leader of the group, liked to read letters from missionaries who had gone to the province of Bengal in India.

BENGAL HAS MANY ORPHANS WHO HAVE BEEN DESERTED BY THEIR PARENTS. THEY ARE STARVING AND THEY SUFFER TERRIBLE THINGS.

SOB, SOB.

DO YOU FEEL DEEPLY SORRY FOR THEM?

YES—I DO.

AGNES CRIES WHEN SHE HEARS STORIES ABOUT MISSIONARIES. SHE MUST HAVE A BIG HEART.

WHY DOES INDIA HAVE SO MANY POOR PEOPLE?

INDIA HAS HAD A HIGHLY CIVILIZED CULTURE THAT DEVELOPED CENTURIES AGO. HOWEVER, THE PEOPLE OF INDIA ARE SUFFERING UNDER ENGLAND'S COLONIAL RULE OF THEIR HOME. AND THERE ARE OTHER FACTORS THAT CREATE PROBLEMS IN INDIAN SOCIETY.

THIS NATION HAS SEVERAL RELIGIONS, INCLUDING HINDUISM, ISLAM AND BUDDHISM. THERE IS ALSO A SOCIAL SYSTEM CALLED THE CASTE SYSTEM THAT IDENTIFIES EVERYONE AS PART OF A CERTAIN SOCIAL GROUP.

SOME GROUPS HAVE JOBS AND FREEDOMS, BUT PEOPLE IN THE LOWEST CASTE HAVE TO BE BEGGARS.

THERE IS A LOT OF CONFLICT BETWEEN THE DIFFERENT RELIGIONS AND THE SOCIAL CASTES, WHICH CONTRIBUTES TO EVERYONE'S MISERY.

THE MISSIONARIES WORKING IN INDIA SAY THAT LOTS OF PEOPLE DIE OF ILLNESSES ON THE STREETS OF INDIA EVERY DAY.

WELL, I WANT TO HELP THE PEOPLE LIVING IN INDIA, TOO.

BUT I DON'T KNOW WHAT TO DO.

GOD, PLEASE TELL ME WHAT TO DO.

29

God listened to her prayer. In 1928, when Agnes was 18, God showed her what he had in mind for her life.

PLEASE HELP THE PEOPLE IN INDIA TO BE FREED FROM THEIR SUFFERINGS AND SHOW ME WHAT I CAN DO FOR THEM.

MY DEAR CHILD AGNES...

YES, LORD?

WHO ARE YOU?

OH!

THERE ARE SO MANY PEOPLE WHO NEED YOUR HELP IN THE WORLD.

LOVE AND CARE FOR THEM WITH THE SAME LOVING SERVICE THAT YOU OFFER ME.

OH, MY FATHER... I WILL OBEY YOU. THANK YOU FOR SHOWING ME A PATH.

YOU HAVE MANY GIFTS, AND YOU WILL SERVE ME BY SERVING THE POOR AND HELPLESS.

At that moment, her heart was filled with fear as well as joy. She prayed until darkness fell, asking for the strength to fulfill her promise.

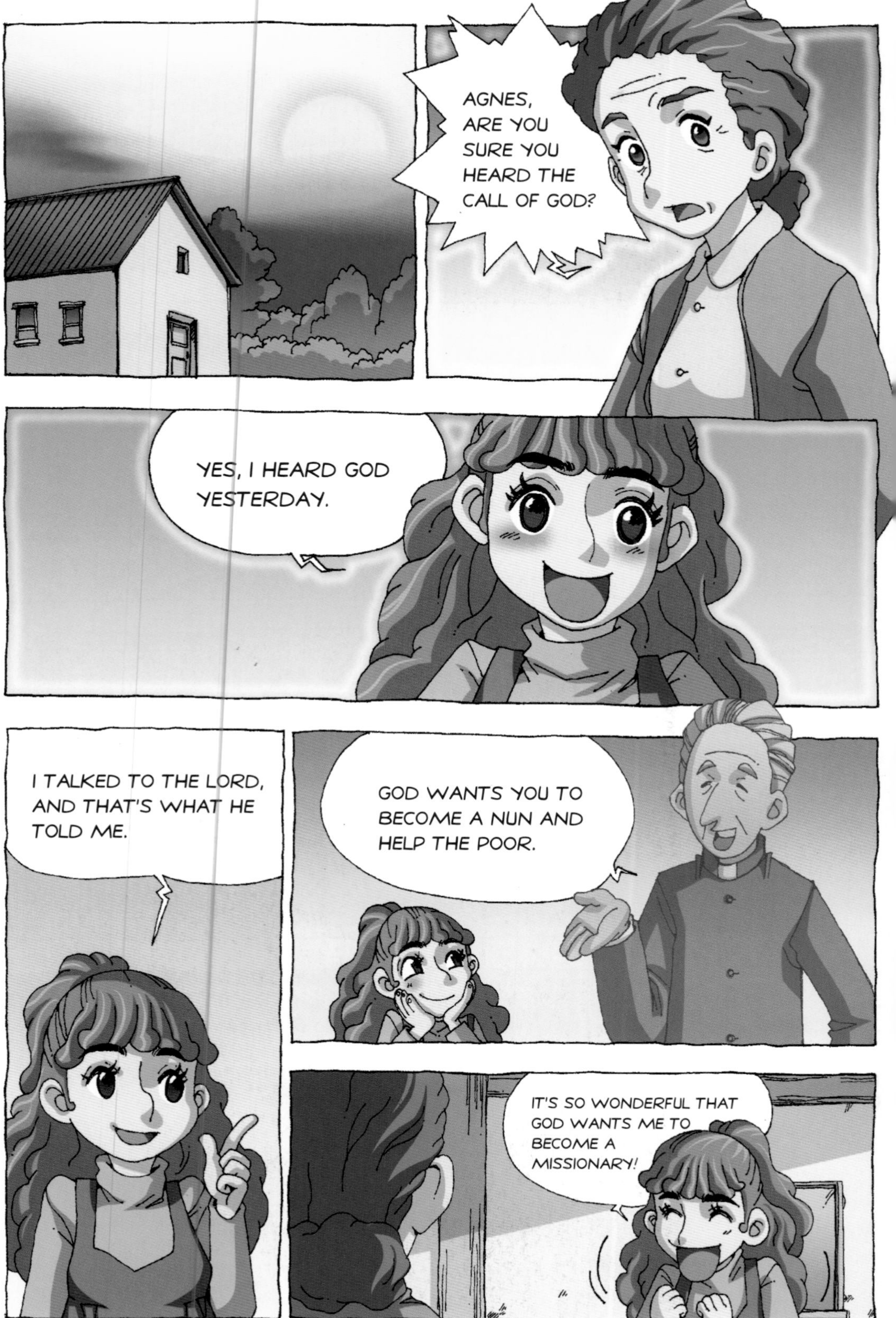
AGNES, ARE YOU SURE YOU HEARD THE CALL OF GOD?
YES, I HEARD GOD YESTERDAY.
I TALKED TO THE LORD, AND THAT'S WHAT HE TOLD ME.
GOD WANTS YOU TO BECOME A NUN AND HELP THE POOR.
IT'S SO WONDERFUL THAT GOD WANTS ME TO BECOME A MISSIONARY!

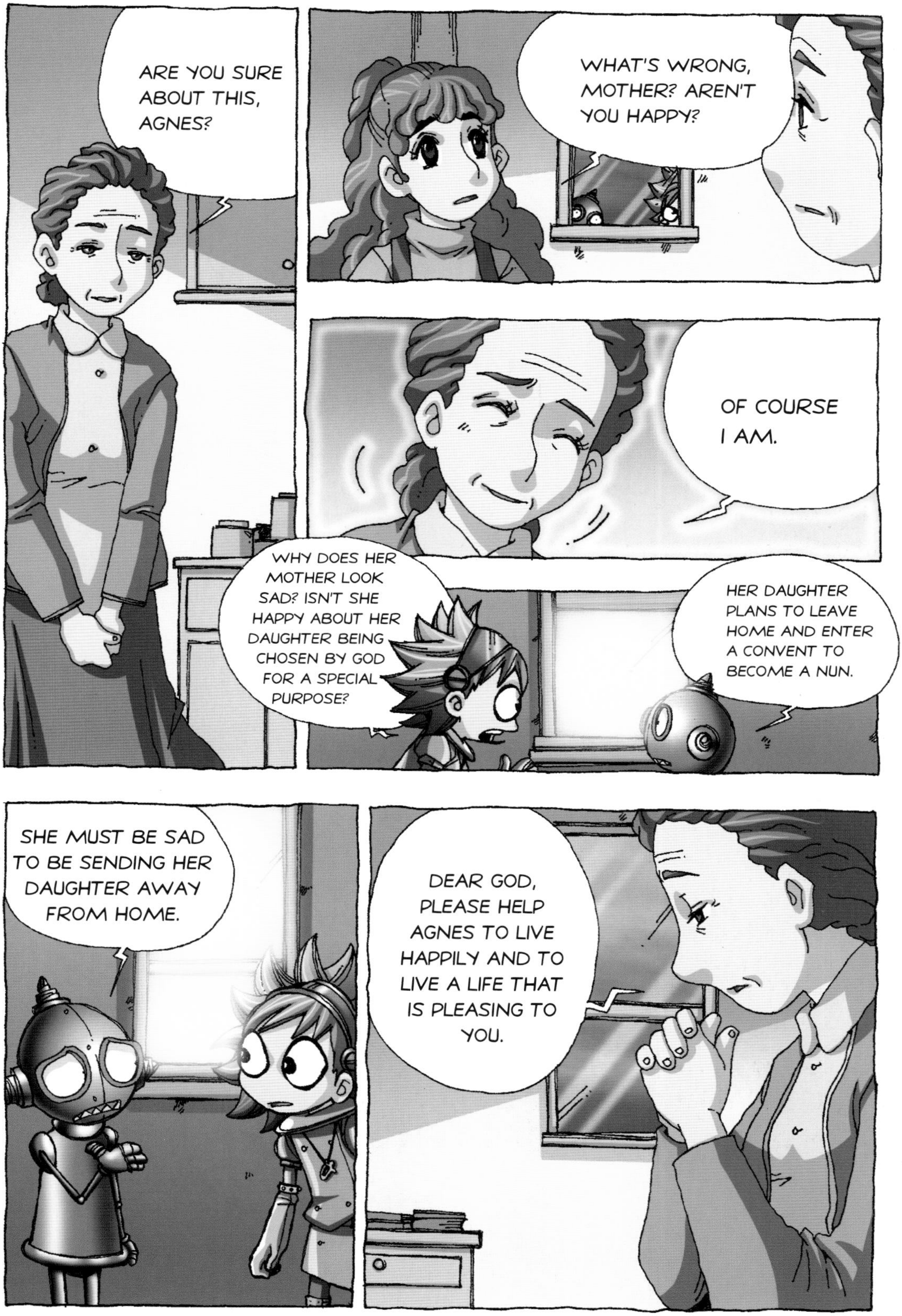
ARE YOU SURE ABOUT THIS, AGNES?
WHAT'S WRONG, MOTHER? AREN'T YOU HAPPY?
OF COURSE I AM.
WHY DOES HER MOTHER LOOK SAD? ISN'T SHE HAPPY ABOUT HER DAUGHTER BEING CHOSEN BY GOD FOR A SPECIAL PURPOSE?
HER DAUGHTER PLANS TO LEAVE HOME AND ENTER A CONVENT TO BECOME A NUN.
SHE MUST BE SAD TO BE SENDING HER DAUGHTER AWAY FROM HOME.
DEAR GOD, PLEASE HELP AGNES TO LIVE HAPPILY AND TO LIVE A LIFE THAT IS PLEASING TO YOU.

That same year, Agnes left for the Loreto convent in Dublin, Ireland. The Sisters of Loreto had a missionary program in India.

PLEASE DON'T CRY, MOTHER. I WILL DO MY BEST TO MAKE YOU PROUD.

YES, I KNOW YOU WILL DO YOUR BEST. YOU ALWAYS DO THE RIGHT THING.

ENTRUST YOURSELF TO GOD AND FOLLOW HIS GUIDANCE IN ALL THINGS.

YES, MOTHER. I WILL REMEMBER.

CHUG CHUG

TAKE GOOD CARE OF MOTHER!

WE WILL. TAKE CARE.

After traveling by several ships and trains, Agnes finally reached Ireland.

The convent for the Sisters of Loreto

The Sisters of Loreto is an international religious order that encourages women to use their skills to help society.

Agnes spent six weeks studying English because the nuns in India spoke English.

THE PROCESS OF BECOMING A NUN IS MADE UP OF FOUR STEPS. COMPLETING THEM CAN TAKE SOME TIME.

After finishing her training, Agnes finally arrived in India on December 1, 1928. Then she went to Calcutta by train on January 6, 1929.

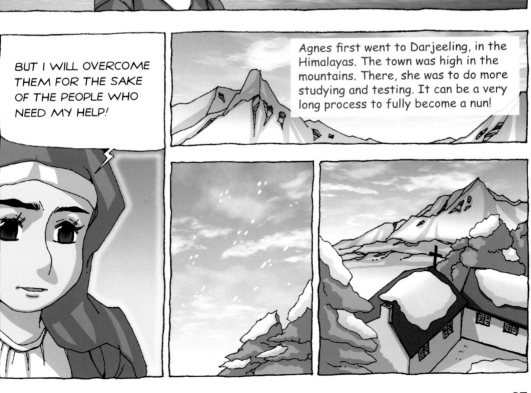

Agnes first went to Darjeeling, in the Himalayas. The town was high in the mountains. There, she was to do more studying and testing. It can be a very long process to fully become a nun!

ACHOO!

She lived and studied in a cold, old Loreto convent.

THE BOOK OF JOB, CHAPTER 3.

Two years later, on May 24, 1931, the day came for her to take her first vows.

The vows are a pledge of dedication to God.

The nuns were given gold rings to wear on the right ring fingers as symbols of their promises to serve God for the rest of their lives.

CONGRATULATIONS, AGNES!

THANK YOU, FATHER!

DID YOU SELECT YOUR NEW NAME?

When taking their vows, nuns can select a new name to honor the saints that inspire them.

YES.

WHAT IS IT?

TERESA.

SAINT THERESA OF LISIEUX WAS THE PATRONESS OF MISSIONARIES. TERESA WANTED TO BE A GOOD MISSIONARY.

EPISODE 3
TEACHING IN CALCUTTA

Sister Teresa was assigned to the Loreto community in eastern Calcutta (today called Kolkata), the biggest city in India.

Loreto's convent in Calcutta

Sister Teresa joined the community to realize her dream of helping the poor and sick. However, she was given an unexpected task.

ARE YOU SURE?

YOU WANT ME TO TEACH CHILDREN AT SCHOOL?

BUT I BECAME A NUN TO HELP THE POOR PEOPLE OF INDIA.

PLEASE THINK ABOUT IT AGAIN.

BUT THERE IS NOTHING I CAN DO.

YOU HAVE TO BE OUTSIDE THE CONVENT TO HELP THE SICK AND POOR, WHICH IS NOT ALLOWED BY THE RULES OF LORETO CONVENT.

TEACHING CHILDREN IS ALSO A PRECIOUS WORK OF SERVICE. I HOPE YOU WILL PERFORM THIS JOB WITH PLEASURE.

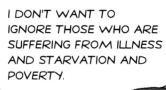

I DON'T WANT TO IGNORE THOSE WHO ARE SUFFERING FROM ILLNESS AND STARVATION AND POVERTY.

HOWEVER, I CAN'T BREAK THE RULES. IT IS ALSO IMPORTANT TO TEACH THE CHILDREN.

Sister Teresa would make no other choice. She taught geography and history to the girls of St. Mary's High School.

Most of the students were from middle class families who didn't live in poverty.

Although Sister Teresa took the job with disappointment, she worked very hard at teaching her students. They followed her with great respect.

In 1944, Mother Teresa became the principal of the school. This left her more peace and quiet.

On the other hand, the situation in Calcutta was getting worse.

On August 15, 1946, a battle erupted between India's Hindus and Muslims, causing many injuries and deaths. Stores closed, and the children at the school had no food.

Thirty-seven years old

44

WHAT AM I DOING HERE WHEN THE POOR PEOPLE OUTSIDE RISK DYING OF STARVATION?

OH GOD, PLEASE TELL ME WHAT CAN I DO FOR THEM.

Finally, Mother Teresa became ill because she so badly wanted to help the poor people.

MOTHER TERESA, I THINK YOU ARE OVERWORKED.

I AGREE. PLEASE, LET US HANDLE THE WORK HERE AND YOU CAN GO SOMEWHERE CALMER TO RECOVER.

NO, I DON'T WANT TO LEAVE... I JUST WANT TO STAY HERE.

IT IS OUR RESPONSIBILITY TO KEEP YOU HEALTHY. PLEASE TAKE SOME TIME TO REST.

WELL...

IF I LEAVE HERE, I MAY NEVER HAVE A CHANCE TO HELP THE PEOPLE OUT THERE.

On September 10, 1946, Mother Teresa traveled to Darjeeling, the town where she had stayed for her training.

....

While traveling on the train, she received another message from God.

DEAR GOD, I CAN'T LEAVE THOSE POOR PEOPLE OF CALCUTTA.

PLEASE ALLOW ME THE COURAGE AND HEALTH TO HELP THEM.

MY DEAR TERESA, OPEN YOUR EYES.

LEAVE EVERYTHING YOU HAVE, AND GO TO YOUR SISTERS AND BROTHERS WHO NEED YOUR HELP.

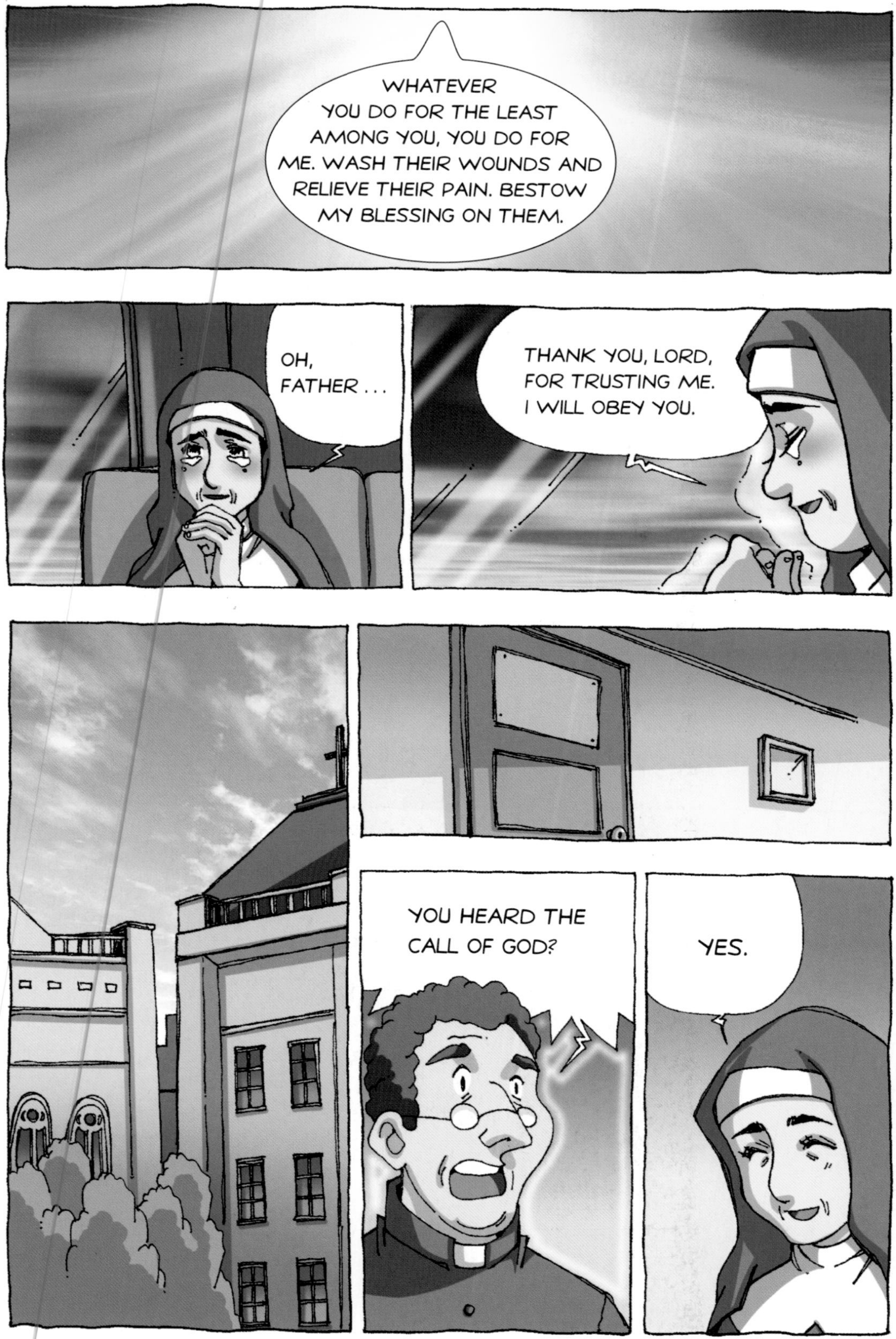
WHATEVER YOU DO FOR THE LEAST AMONG YOU, YOU DO FOR ME. WASH THEIR WOUNDS AND RELIEVE THEIR PAIN. BESTOW MY BLESSING ON THEM.
OH, FATHER . . .
THANK YOU, LORD, FOR TRUSTING ME. I WILL OBEY YOU.
YOU HEARD THE CALL OF GOD?
YES.

GOD SAID I SHOULD GO TO THE POOR. THOUGH HE HAS ALREADY CALLED ME TO COME TO INDIA, THIS WAS A CALL WITHIN A CALL. NOW I KNOW WHAT I SHOULD BE DOING IN INDIA.

GOD HAS FINALLY SHOWN YOU WHAT HE WANTS YOU TO DO.

IF GOD WANTS YOU TO LEAVE THE CONVENT,

YOU WILL HAVE TO GET PERMISSION FROM THE CHURCH. I WILL RECOMMEND YOU TO THE ARCHBISHOP.

THANK YOU, FATHER.

It was forbidden for Loreto nuns to live outside the convent at that time. If Mother Teresa obtained permission from the church, she would become the first nun to do so in the 300-year history of the Loreto convent.

Obtaining permission was a long and complicated process. First, she needed the approval of the archbishop of India.

Eventually, her request had to be approved by the highest authority in the Catholic Church—the pope in Rome.

Dear Father, I heard the voice of God ordering me to help the alienated in India. I want to stay with the poor of Calcutta and spread Jesus's love among them. Please allow me to leave the convent and stay with them.

I SHOULDN'T BE NERVOUS. I WILL JUST TRY TO RELAX AND WAIT FOR THE RESPONSE.

In April 1948, she got the answer she wanted at last. Pope Pius XII had given her permission to stay out of the convent for only one year, starting in August.

Mother Teresa had waited for this letter for two years.

THANK YOU! THANK YOU SO MUCH.

HURRAY!

ALL READY!

I AM HAPPY FOR YOU BECAUSE YOU CAN FINALLY SERVE GOD AS YOU WANT.

I CAN LIVE MY DREAM, THANKS TO YOUR HELP.

GOOD-BYE, AND TAKE CARE.

August 18, 1948

Teresa began her journey around India to help the poor and the sick.

NOW, WE WILL FINALLY BE ABLE TO SEE THE WORK OF MOTHER TERESA!

EPISODE 4
SCHOOL UNDER A GUAVA TREE

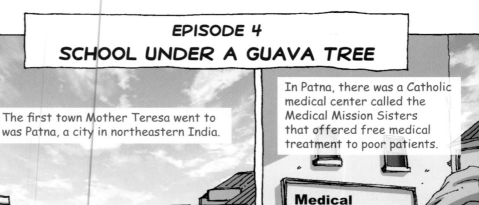

The first town Mother Teresa went to was Patna, a city in northeastern India.

In Patna, there was a Catholic medical center called the Medical Mission Sisters that offered free medical treatment to poor patients.

Medical Mission Sisters

ARE YOU SURE YOU WANT TO WORK HERE?

YES, I AM SURE. I KNOW YOU ARE TERRIBLY BUSY, BUT PLEASE LET ME WORK AND LEARN FROM YOU.

WELL...

LEARNING MEDICAL SKILLS IS EXTREMELY HARD WORK. IT MAY TAKE MORE THAN A YEAR TO LEARN THE BASICS.

IT MAY BE TOO HARD FOR YOU.

RATHER, FIND EASIER WAYS, LIKE FUND RAISING...

I NEED TO LEARN MEDICAL SKILLS.

I WANT TO HELP THE SICK AND POOR. MEDICAL CARE IS JUST AS IMPORTANT AS FOOD.

I COULD NEVER FORGIVE MYSELF IF I HAD TO WATCH THEM SUFFER JUST BECAUSE I DON'T KNOW HOW TO HELP.

I WANT TO BE LIKE LIGHT AND SALT FOR THE PEOPLE WHO NEED ME. PLEASE TEACH ME HOW TO CARE FOR THEM. I WILL DO MY BEST.

YOU HAVE GREAT PASSION!

ALL RIGHT. I WILL TEACH YOU AS MUCH AS I CAN.

THANK YOU!

Mother Teresa learned how to care for the patients at the Holy Family Hospital.

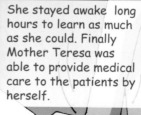

She stayed awake long hours to learn as much as she could. Finally Mother Teresa was able to provide medical care to the patients by herself.

HOW DO YOU FEEL NOW?

MUCH BETTER! YOU'VE BEEN AN ANGEL!

I'M READY!

After six months of studying medical treatment at the hospital, she moved back to Calcutta.

December 1948, Motijhil, a slum of Calcutta

Motijhil means "Pearl Lake," but this poor area of Calcutta was full of disease, ignorance, and corruption.

Naked children wandered in the streets without supervision.

The majority of people in Motijhil lived in shoddy houses and earned just enough money to eat by doing cleaning jobs in Calcutta. Almost every household had a sick person.

THIS PLACE IS REALLY MISERABLE.

I THOUGHT I WAS READY. BUT NOW I'M NOT SURE WHERE TO START.

I HAVE NO FRIENDS OR ORGANIZATION TO HELP ME.

BUT I WILL NOT BE AFRAID. GOD IS WITH ME.

OH, LORD! I HAVE COME HERE TO SPREAD LOVE AMONG THE PEOPLE HERE.

PLEASE, LET ME SHARE YOUR HEART AND WILL. AMEN.

I MUST CHEER UP. I WILL START A NEW LIFE WITH THEM, FOLLOWING GOD'S WILL!

THE BIGGEST REASON THAT PEOPLE ARE POOR HERE IS THAT THEY WERE NOT EDUCATED. I WILL START BY LIGHTING THE SPARK OF KNOWLEDGE TO ELIMINATE THE DARKNESS OF IGNORANCE.

The first thing Mother Teresa did was to teach poor children who had no other chance to be educated.

She knew that without education children would have difficulty finding jobs when they grew up.

60

HEY, HOW ABOUT PLAYING SCHOOL WITH ME?

WHAT? WHAT IS SCHOOL?

WOW, YOU WILL TEACH US HOW TO COUNT NUMBERS? AND HOW TO WRITE?

SCHOOL IS LEARNING ABOUT NUMBERS AND LETTERS.

SURE—I WILL TEACH WHATEVER YOU WANT TO KNOW.

WOW! FUN!

Mother Teresa started teaching the local children. With no blackboards or chalk, she had to write in the sand with a stick. Sitting under a guava tree, she started her first elementary school class.

NOW, LET'S RECITE THE MULTIPLES OF THREE!

The conditions were bad, but Mother Teresa and the children were as passionate about learning as the teachers and students of any other school.

OKAY!

3, 6, 9, 12, 15 . . .

I ONLY KNOW HOW TO COUNT TO 10.

UMM . . .

. . .18, 21, 24, 27, 30.

HURRAY!

WOW! THAT LOOKS FUN.

LET US JOIN, PLEASE.

More and more children joined the school as they heard about it.

Their parents began to donate chalk and blackboards, despite their limited funds.

Slowly, Teresa's school became established.

ANYBODY WHO HAS A SICK FAMILY MEMBER, RAISE YOUR HAND, PLEASE.

Then Mother Teresa began the second step of her volunteering work.

I CAN'T BELIEVE THIS! THERE ARE SO MANY SICK PEOPLE TO BE CARED FOR. I SHOULD START PROVIDING MEDICAL HELP AS SOON AS POSSIBLE.

I WILL VISIT THE FAMILIES WITH SICK PEOPLE. STUDENTS, I WANT 10 OF YOU TO WAIT FOR ME AFTER CLASS EACH DAY.

YES.

Mother Teresa visited her students' families after school each day.

YOU WILL GET BETTER SOON IF YOU USE THIS OINTMENT THREE TIMES A DAY.

ARE YOU GIVING ME THIS MEDICINE FREE OF CHARGE? I CAN'T ACCEPT IT.

DON'T WORRY. I HAVE PLENTY OF MEDICATION.

I DON'T KNOW HOW TO THANK YOU FOR THIS.

THANK YOU, MOTHER.

I TRIED TO EASE THEIR WORRY. REALLY I HAVE ONLY A FEW MEDICATIONS. BUT THERE ARE SO MANY ILL PEOPLE.

Mother Teresa's biggest concern was obtaining money to buy enough medications to help the sick.

She had been using the medications from the medical center in Patna. But there were so many ill people in the city that she needed many more drugs.

So Mother Teresa visited hospitals and pharmacies in the evenings to request more drugs to treat patients.

IF YOU DONATE SOME DRUGS FOR THE POOR, THAT WILL BE A BIG HELP TO THEM.

OH, DEAR.

LOOK AT THESE TERRIBLY SWOLLEN FEET.

THAT'S TOO BAD. I HAVE SO MANY THINGS TO DO TODAY...

TERESA, YOU CAN'T BE LAZY OR TIRED. THERE ARE SO MANY WHO NEED YOUR HELP.

I'D BETTER GET STARTED. OUCH.

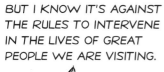

LIMP LIMP

I WISH I COULD HELP HER.

BUT I KNOW IT'S AGAINST THE RULES TO INTERVENE IN THE LIVES OF GREAT PEOPLE WE ARE VISITING.

SIGH!

WHERE ARE YOU GOING?

ARE YOU TRYING TO TAKE MEDICATIONS TO HER?

WELL, I WAS ONLY GOING TO GIVE HER A FEW DRUGS . . .

BUT THAT IS AGAINST THE RULES!

HEY, DON'T YOU FEEL SORRY FOR HER?

STILL, YOU MUST FOLLOW THE RULES.

YOU ARE A BRUTE!

She worked hard every day despite many challenges.

Mother Teresa received some help from others.

ARE YOU REALLY DONATING MEDICATIONS?

YES, INDEED.

MANY PEOPLE ARE SO MOVED BY YOUR DEDICATION THAT THEY HAVE COMBINED THEIR MONEY TO HELP YOU.

THANK YOU SO MUCH. MAY GOD BE WITH YOU.

I DON'T DESERVE YOUR BLESSING.

PLEASE, COME INSIDE.

I HAVEN'T SEEN YOU IN A LONG TIME, MOTHER TERESA.

AREN'T YOU MY FORMER STUDENT SUBASHINI DAS? HOW HAVE YOU BEEN?

WE HEARD ABOUT YOUR WORK FROM THE NUNS AT LORETO.

I HEARD YOU LEFT THE CONVENT TO HELP THE SICK AND POOR. I WANTED TO HELP YOU. SO I HAVE BEEN LOOKING FOR SUPPORTERS.

Subashini Das had been one of Teresa's students at St. Mary's High School.

SUBASHINI...

Subashini Das loved and respected Mother Teresa. She joined Teresa in her work, and later changed her name to Sister Agnes.

SISTER, DO YOU KNOW WHAT I WANT TO BE?

WHAT?

71

I WANT TO BECOME A WONDERFUL NUN LIKE YOU.

SURE, I WILL.

I WILL FIND YOU WHEN I GROW UP. I HOPE YOU WILL TEACH ME THEN.

DO YOU WANT TO WORK WITH ME HERE?

YES, MOTHER. I WANT TO HELP THE POOR WITH YOU. PLEASE LET ME WORK HERE.

COMPARE MY CLOTHING WITH YOUR BEAUTIFUL CLOTHES. CAN YOU LIVE WITHOUT MONEY? YOU HAVE TO DEDICATE YOURSELF TO YOUR NEIGHBORS AND YOUR GOD. ALSO, YOU MUST BE PREPARED TO GIVE YOUR LOVE, YOUR TIME, AND YOUR MONEY.

I THOUGHT ABOUT IT FOR A LONG TIME AND I AM READY NOW.

SHE IS LIKE ME WHEN I LEFT THE CONVENT.

ALL RIGHT. YOU CAN WORK WITH ME STARTING TOMORROW.

I WILL DO MY BEST!

One month later

FINISHED!

HURRAY! WE'RE DONE!

ALL THIS WAS POSSIBLE THANKS TO THE FINANCIAL SUPPORT THAT YOU HAVE RAISED.

REALLY?

MOTHER...

ARE YOU REALLY TAKING CARE OF SICK PEOPLE FREE OF CHARGE?

OF COURSE!

MY WIFE HAS A HIGH FEVER. COUGH. COUGH.

YOU LOOK ILL, TOO.

WE WILL TREAT YOU FIRST. THEN BRING YOUR WIFE HERE.

HOW COULD I ASK YOU TO TREAT ME WHEN MY WIFE IS ILL?

DON'T WORRY. WE HAVE PLENTY OF MEDICINE, THANKS TO SOME GOOD PEOPLE. PLEASE BRING HER HERE.

REALLY?

I WILL BE BACK SOON!

HE SEEMS TO FEEL BETTER ALREADY!

Teresa's free medical center was crowded with patients.

Surrounded by people needing her help, Mother Teresa didn't rest very often. However, knowing that she was helping people made her happy.

She also had a growing number of supporters.

Several volunteer workers, including many of her former students, came to help Mother Teresa.

LET'S TAKE TURNS RESTING AND SLEEPING, BECAUSE WE ARE SO BUSY.

WE ARE FINE. HOW CAN WE HAVE A BREAK WHILE YOU ARE WORKING SO HARD?

EPISODE 5
MISSIONARIES OF CHARITY

One year later

GOD, PLEASE ALLOW US TO TAKE CARE OF MORE PEOPLE TODAY. AMEN.

AMEN.

WELL, LET'S WORK HARDER TODAY THAN EVER.

KNOCK KNOCK

WHO IS VISITING AT THIS EARLY HOUR?

HOW ARE YOU, TERESA?

WELCOME, FATHER. WE HAVEN'T SEEN EACH OTHER FOR A LONG TIME.

GOOD NEWS?

IT IS EARLY IN THE MORNING, BUT I WANTED TO TELL YOU THE GOOD NEWS AS SOON AS POSSIBLE.

THE VATICAN DECIDED TO APPROVE YOUR WORK AS A NEW RELIGIOUS ORDER.

OUR GROUP HAS BEEN APPROVED BY THE CHURCH? THAT'S WONDERFUL!

This meant that their work with the poor would now be regarded as an official, approved activity of the Vatican. It was a great honor for Mother Teresa.

The archbishop of India was moved by her dedication to the poor and sick.

CONGRATULATIONS, SISTERS!

I COULDN'T DO IT WITHOUT YOU ALL. THANK YOU SO MUCH.

. . . .

THAT'S GREAT!

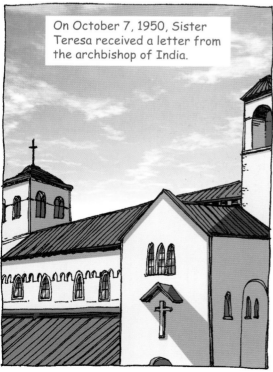

On October 7, 1950, Sister Teresa received a letter from the archbishop of India.

ON BEHALF OF POPE PAUL VI, I APPROVE THE MISSIONARIES OF CHARITY AS AN OFFICIAL ACTIVITY OF THE CATHOLIC HURCH.

MISSIONARIES OF CHARITY . . . THAT IS A GOOD NAME.

YES, IT MEANS THAT WE WILL STRIVE TO SPREAD THE LOVE OF GOD AMONG THE POOREST PEOPLE AND HELP THEM.

PLEASE CONTINUE TO HELP AND SERVE GOD'S POOR CHILDREN, TERESA.

GOD BLESS YOU.

YOU ARE A FAITHFUL SERVANT OF JESUS CHRIST.

THE GLORY IS GOD'S.

PRAISE GOD!

Ten volunteer workers, including Subashini Das, became nuns in the new order of the Missionaries of Charity.

FOR YOU!

They went back to their work right after the announcement.

YOU ARE DRESSED LIKE MOTHER TERESA. IT SUITS YOU!

YOU ARE GRINNING EAR TO EAR.

PLEASE, CALL ME SISTER AGNES.

HA, HA, HA.

HA, HA.

THEY ARE SO HAPPY TO BE OFFICIAL NUNS.

YEAH. IT MUST FEEL GOOD TO HELP PEOPLE.

SNIFF, SNIFF!

UGH, WHAT IS THAT SMELL?

IT SMELLS PRETTY ROTTEN.

MAYBE SOMEONE HID SOME ROTTEN FOOD AROUND HERE.

NO, NO. LOOK AT THE FEET. IT MUST BE SOMETHING OUT THERE.

OH, NO!

IT SMELLS REALLY BAD.

OH DEAR, HER CONDITION IS REALLY BAD . . .

WE HAVE TO GO TO THE HOSPITAL AS SOON AS POSSIBLE!

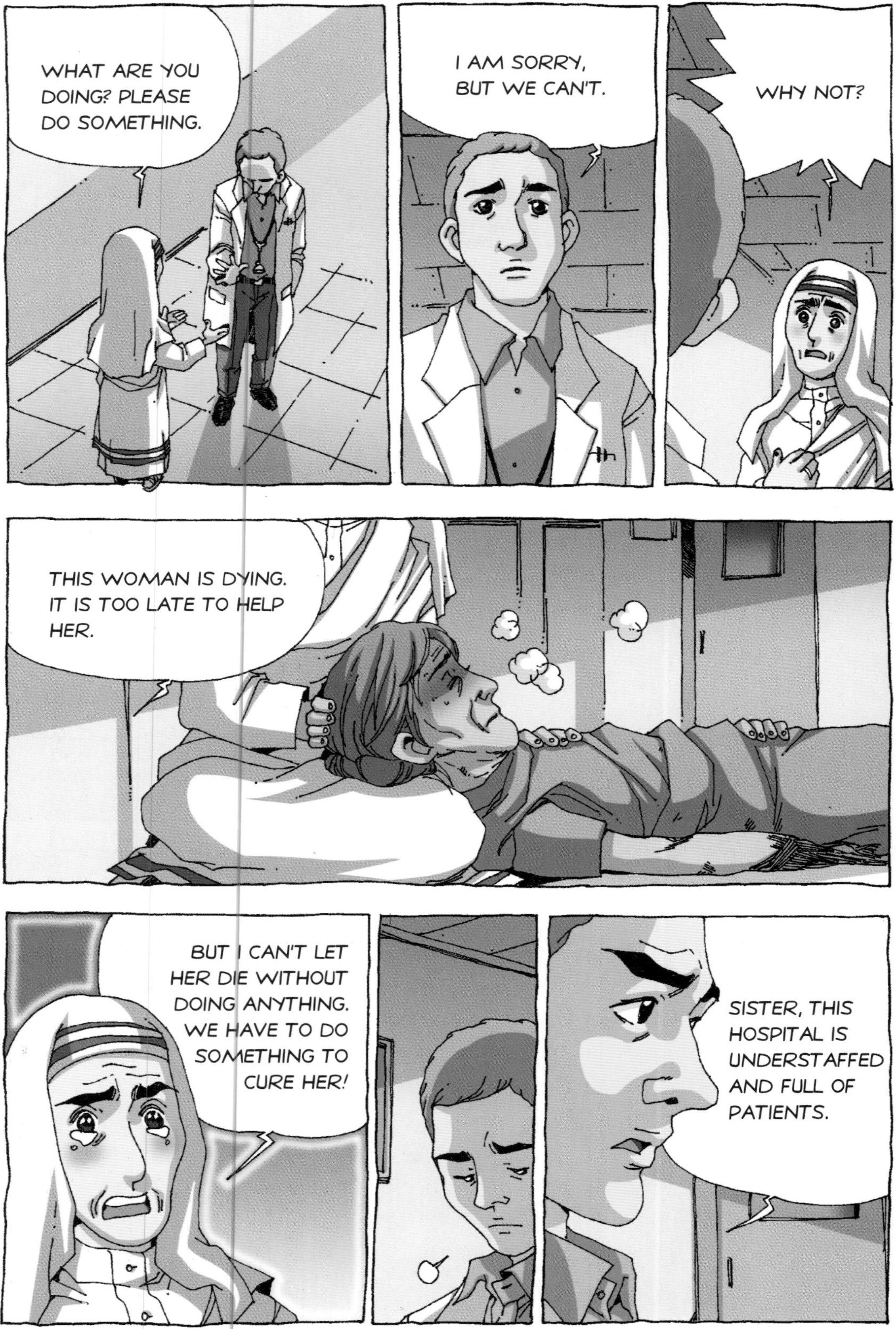
WHAT ARE YOU DOING? PLEASE DO SOMETHING.
I AM SORRY, BUT WE CAN'T.
WHY NOT?
THIS WOMAN IS DYING. IT IS TOO LATE TO HELP HER.
BUT I CAN'T LET HER DIE WITHOUT DOING ANYTHING. WE HAVE TO DO SOMETHING TO CURE HER!
SISTER, THIS HOSPITAL IS UNDERSTAFFED AND FULL OF PATIENTS.

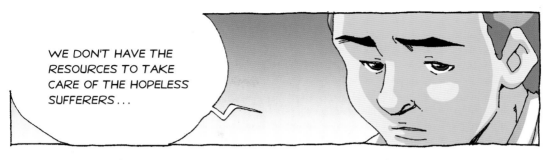

WE DON'T HAVE THE RESOURCES TO TAKE CARE OF THE HOPELESS SUFFERERS...

BUT... BUT...

SISTER...

DON'T WORRY, SISTER.

I KNOW THAT I WILL NOT RECOVER. BUT I AM NOT SAD.

I HAVE NEVER BEEN LOVED DURING MY WHOLE LIFE.

I EVEN DON'T KNOW WHO MY PARENTS ARE.

BUT WHEN I SAW YOU CRYING FOR ME, I REALIZED THAT I AM ABLE TO BE LOVED.

I DON'T WANT ANYTHING MORE. THANK YOU, SISTER.

SISTER . . .

OH, LORD, PLEASE ALLOW THIS WOMAN TO JOIN YOU IN HEAVEN.

SOB SOB SOB

I HAVE MADE A DECISION.

WHAT IS IT?

I WANT TO PROVIDE A PLACE FOR DYING PEOPLE TO HAVE COMPASSIONATE, LOVING CARE FOR THE FINAL DAYS OF THEIR LIVES.

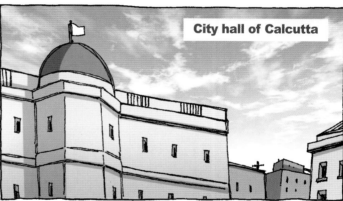

City hall of Calcutta

Mother Teresa met the mayor of the city and asked for his help.

....

I UNDERSTAND WHAT YOU ARE TALKING ABOUT. BUT THERE ARE LOTS OF PEOPLE DYING ON THE STREETS OF CALCUTTA EVERY DAY.

WE CANNOT AFFORD TO TAKE CARE OF THEM ALL.

HE DOES NOT TAKE ME SERIOUSLY, JUST AS I FEARED.

DON'T WORRY. PLEASE JUST ALLOW US A PLACE WHERE WE CAN TAKE CARE OF DYING PEOPLE. WE WILL HANDLE THE REST OF THE DETAILS.

OKAY, IF YOU ARE SURE.

HOW LUCKY I AM! I CAN ADDRESS ONE OF THE BIGGEST PROBLEMS EASILY.

The mayor let them use an abandoned temple. The temple was originally for Kali.

KALI IS A HINDU GODDESS WORSHIPED BY MANY HINDUS IN INDIA.

MY GOODNESS!

In August, Mother Teresa opened the Nirmal Hriday Home for the Dying to be a special hospital for dying patients. Teresa was 42 years old.

Nirmal Hriday means "pure heart."

OH!

The patients who entered the center were chronically ill, meaning that there was no cure for their illnesses. Most of them were homeless, so they had no family or friends to care for them.

THE SISTERS MUST HAVE VERY BIG HEARTS TO HELP THESE PEOPLE ALL DAY.

YES.

The nuns took care of the dying people and made them as comfortable as possible.

They were cheerful even when the job was upsetting and patients did not regain their strength.

Thanks to selfless efforts of the nuns and other volunteers, the patients' spirits improved even when their diseases weren't.

However, the sick patients couldn't stay long because they were so ill.

OH!

OH!

GIVE HIM SOME PAINKILLERS, PLEASE.

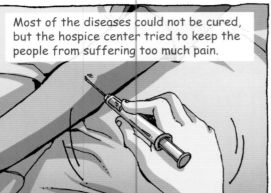

Most of the diseases could not be cured, but the hospice center tried to keep the people from suffering too much pain.

I DON'T FEEL THE PAIN ANY MORE. THANK YOU!

BUT I AM SLEEPY NOW. I PROBABLY WON'T LIVE MUCH LONGER.

YOU WILL HAVE A HAPPY LIFE IN HEAVEN DESPITE YOUR SUFFERINGS ON EARTH.

YES. I WILL WATCH YOU FROM HEAVEN.

LET'S PRAY.
FATHER, PLEASE
GIVE PEACE TO
THIS POOR MAN...

Many patients were able to die peacefully thanks to the nuns' care and kindness.

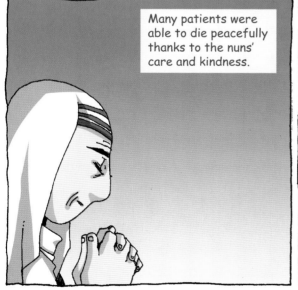

So the Nirmal Hriday was established by the efforts of Mother Teresa.

EPISODE 6
MOTHER OF ORPHANS

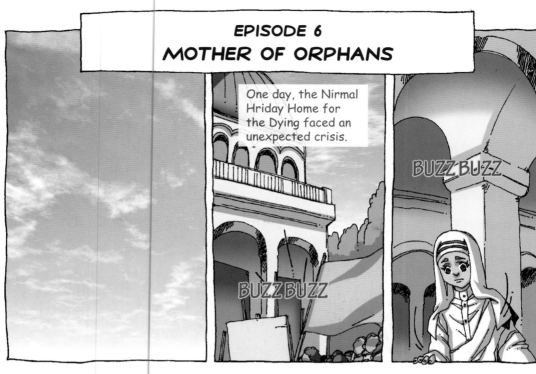

One day, the Nirmal Hriday Home for the Dying faced an unexpected crisis.

BUZZ BUZZ

BUZZ BUZZ

GASP!

MOTHER TERESA! SISTERS!

. . . .

LOOK OUTSIDE! WE ARE IN BIG TROUBLE!

YOU MUST LEAVE THE TEMPLE RIGHT NOW!

YOU HAVE DISGRACED OUR SACRED TEMPLE TO KALI. LEAVE THIS PLACE AS SOON AS POSSIBLE!

YOU CHANGED THIS SACRED TEMPLE INTO A PLACE FOR THE DEAD AND THE DYING.

YOU HEATHENS MUST LEAVE NOW!

THEY THINK WE DISGRACED THEIR TEMPLE.

DON'T WORRY. I WILL HANDLE THIS.

HUAAAA

BAD PEOPLE! THEY'RE TRYING TO FORCE THEM OUT INSTEAD OF HELPING THEM.

I WILL NOT LET YOU DO IT, YOU WICKED PEOPLE!

INITIATING ROBO-TRANSFORM . . .

HERE COMES ROBO-MAN!

STOP THAT NOW!

WHAT?

DID YOU HEAR SOMETHING?

I THINK I DID, BUT . . .

MMPH . . . UNTIE . . . ME.

I TOLD YOU—WE ARE NOT ALLOWED TO INTERVENE INTO THE LIVES OF GREAT PEOPLE WE VISIT!

SHE IS THE PERSON IN CHARGE OF THIS PLACE! GET RID OF HER!

I UNDERSTAND HOW YOU FEEL.

BUT WE CAN'T LET YOUR BROTHERS AND SISTERS DIE ALONE WITHOUT APPROPRIATE CARE.

YOU SHOULD SEE THE PATIENTS BEFORE DEMANDING WE LEAVE THIS PLACE.

WE KNOW WHAT YOUR TRUE INTENTIONS ARE!

YOU JUST WANT TO DISGRACE OUR GODS! YOU DO NOT CARE ABOUT THE SICK PEOPLE!

NO, NOT AT ALL. YOU WILL SEE.

I DON'T BELIEVE YOU!

I WILL HAVE TO SEE IT WITH MY OWN EYES.

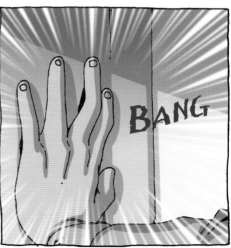

BANG

UGH!

THIS . . . IS TERRIBLE.

WE DO NOT SPARE ANY EFFORTS TO TAKE CARE OF DYING PEOPLE HERE.

IF WE LEAVE THEM, THEY WILL DIE ALONE AND IN PAIN.

PLEASE, LET US USE THIS TEMPLE FOR THEM.

WELL . . .

The representative of the demonstrators told the others what he had seen in the temple. They turned pale while listening to him describe the sufferings of the sick people.

IF WE MAKE THE NUNS LEAVE, OUR MOTHERS AND SISTERS WILL HAVE TO TAKE CARE OF THE DYING PEOPLE INSTEAD.

WELL, LET'S GO HOME AND THINK ABOUT IT.

OKAY.

THANK YOU, GOD, FOR THEIR, UNDERSTANDING AND COOPERATION.

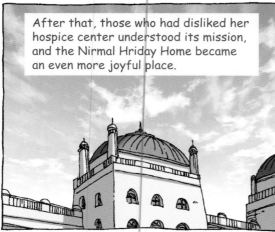

After that, those who had disliked her hospice center understood its mission, and the Nirmal Hriday Home became an even more joyful place.

The good works of Mother Teresa became known throughout India thanks to the newspapers and television.

Many people began to support her order by giving her money and medical supplies.

WE CAN NOW GIVE MEDICAL SUPPORT TO MORE PATIENTS, THANKS TO OUR MANY SUPPORTERS!

People were curious what she would do next.

SISTER, DO YOU HAVE ANY PLANS OTHER THAN THE HOSPICE CENTER?

WELL...

I WANT TO PROVIDE ORPHANS WITH A PLACE TO STAY.

India had a lot of orphans who were abandoned by their parents because of poverty.

Many of them begged or rummaged through garbage cans on the street for food.

And they slept outside in cardboard boxes at night.

They suffered from malnutrition and illnesses. Many children died on the streets without receiving any help.

GET UP!

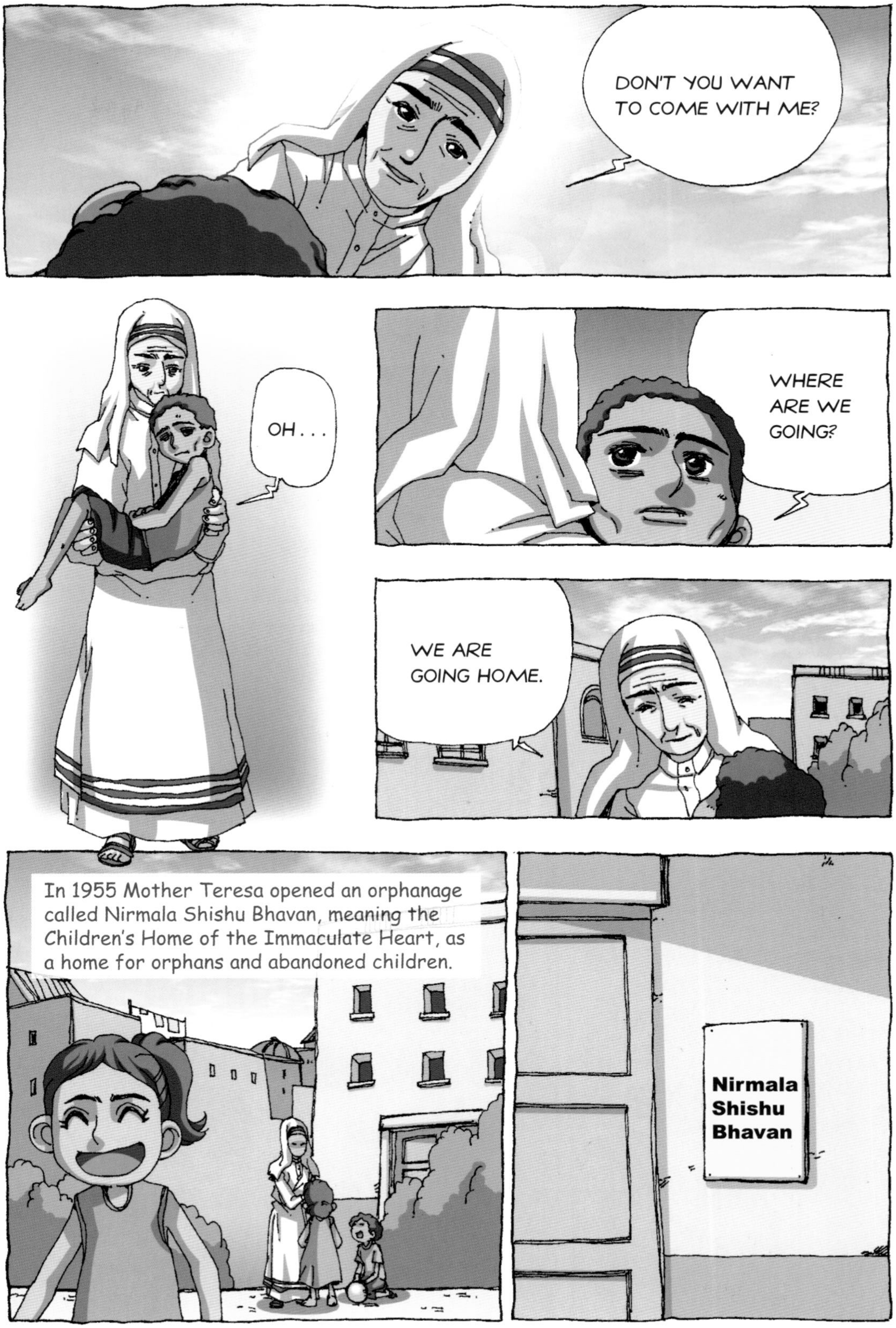
DON'T YOU WANT TO COME WITH ME?
OH . . .
WHERE ARE WE GOING?
WE ARE GOING HOME.
In 1955 Mother Teresa opened an orphanage called Nirmala Shishu Bhavan, meaning the Children's Home of the Immaculate Heart, as a home for orphans and abandoned children.
Nirmala Shishu Bhavan

The children could finally eat until they were full and receive medical care when it was needed.

These children were also able to go to school. The homeless children were given a home.

However, Mother Teresa's priority in operating the orphanage was helping them to be adopted.

She knew that nothing can replace parents' love for their children.

THIS IS THE BOY I TOLD YOU ABOUT.

WE WANT YOU TO BE OUR SON!

THESE PEOPLE WILL GIVE YOU A GOOD HOME. BEHAVE YOURSELF AND RESPECT THEM.

SISTERS... THANK YOU VERY MUCH!

IF YOU HADN'T TAKEN ME IN, I WOULD HAVE STARVED OR DIED ON THE STREETS.

YOU SAVED MY LIFE. GOD BLESS YOU.

The orphanage gave many orphans a new chance at life.

MANY OF THE CHILDREN WHO WERE ADOPTED LATER BECAME VOLUNTEERS FOR MOTHER TERESA WHEN THEY GREW UP.

I GUESS SHE DID MAKE A BIG DIFFERENCE TO THOSE KIDS.

Two years later, in 1957, Mother Teresa was visited by unexpected guests.

KNOCK KNOCK

WHO IS IT?

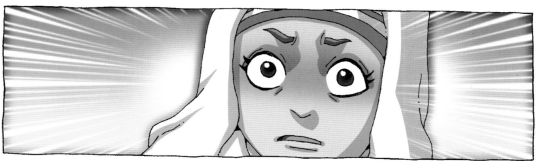

. . . .

IT'S A MONSTER!

EPISODE 7
THE LEPER COLONY

WHAT IS HAPPENING?

THESE PEOPLE HAVE LEPROSY.

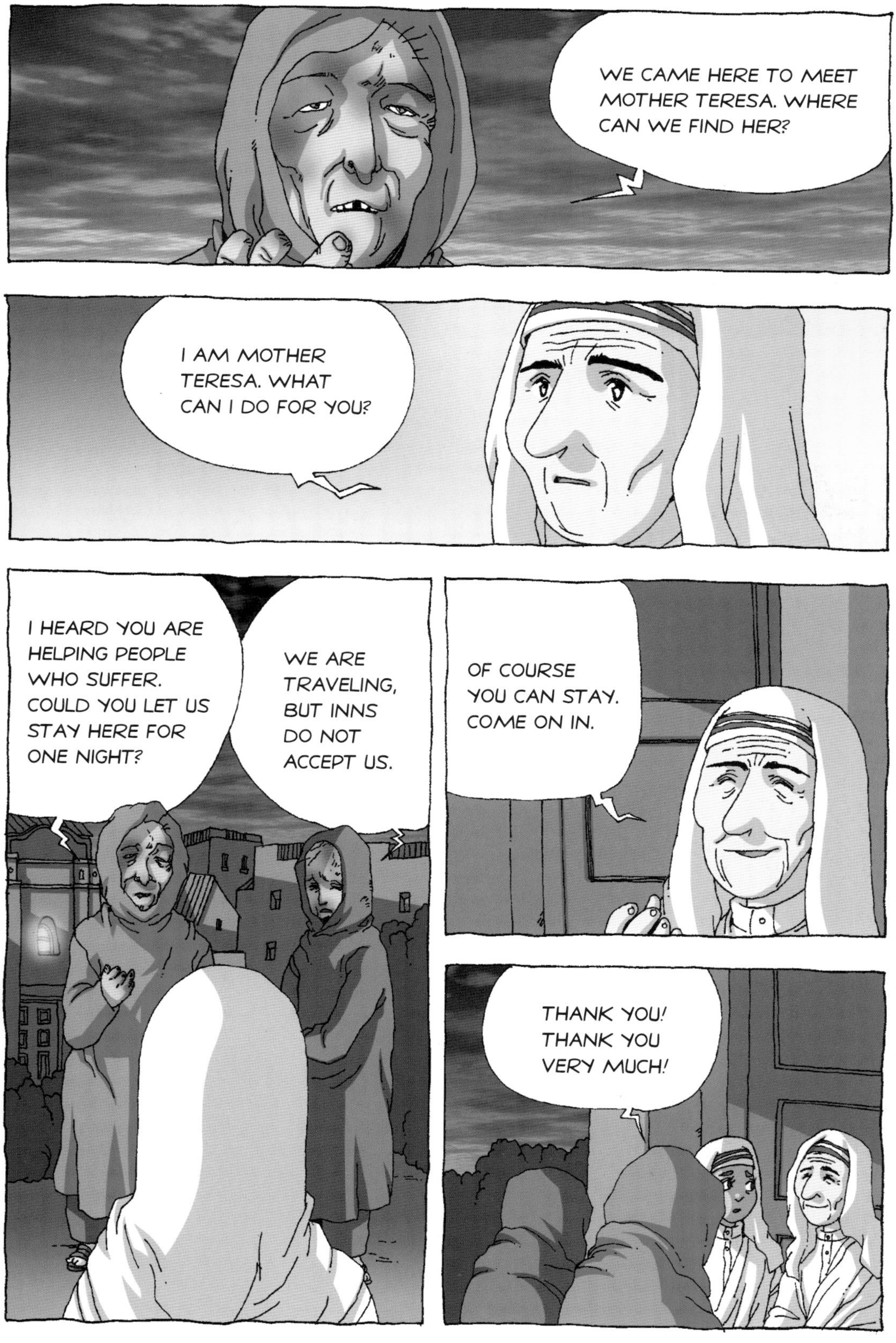
WE CAME HERE TO MEET MOTHER TERESA. WHERE CAN WE FIND HER?
I AM MOTHER TERESA. WHAT CAN I DO FOR YOU?
I HEARD YOU ARE HELPING PEOPLE WHO SUFFER. COULD YOU LET US STAY HERE FOR ONE NIGHT?
WE ARE TRAVELING, BUT INNS DO NOT ACCEPT US.
OF COURSE YOU CAN STAY. COME ON IN.
THANK YOU! THANK YOU VERY MUCH!

BOY, THEY LOOK STRANGE. WHAT'S WRONG WITH THEM?

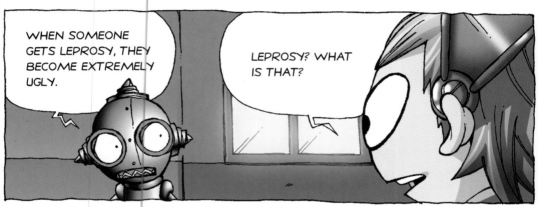

WHEN SOMEONE GETS LEPROSY, THEY BECOME EXTREMELY UGLY.

LEPROSY? WHAT IS THAT?

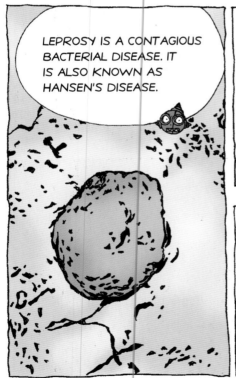

LEPROSY IS A CONTAGIOUS BACTERIAL DISEASE. IT IS ALSO KNOWN AS HANSEN'S DISEASE.

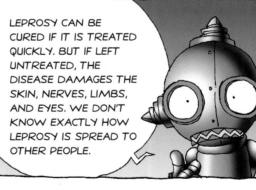

LEPROSY CAN BE CURED IF IT IS TREATED QUICKLY. BUT IF LEFT UNTREATED, THE DISEASE DAMAGES THE SKIN, NERVES, LIMBS, AND EYES. WE DON'T KNOW EXACTLY HOW LEPROSY IS SPREAD TO OTHER PEOPLE.

FOR MOST OF HISTORY, PEOPLE BELIEVED THAT THEY COULD CATCH LEPROSY BY TOUCHING A LEPER'S SKIN OR CLOTHING.

WHAT?

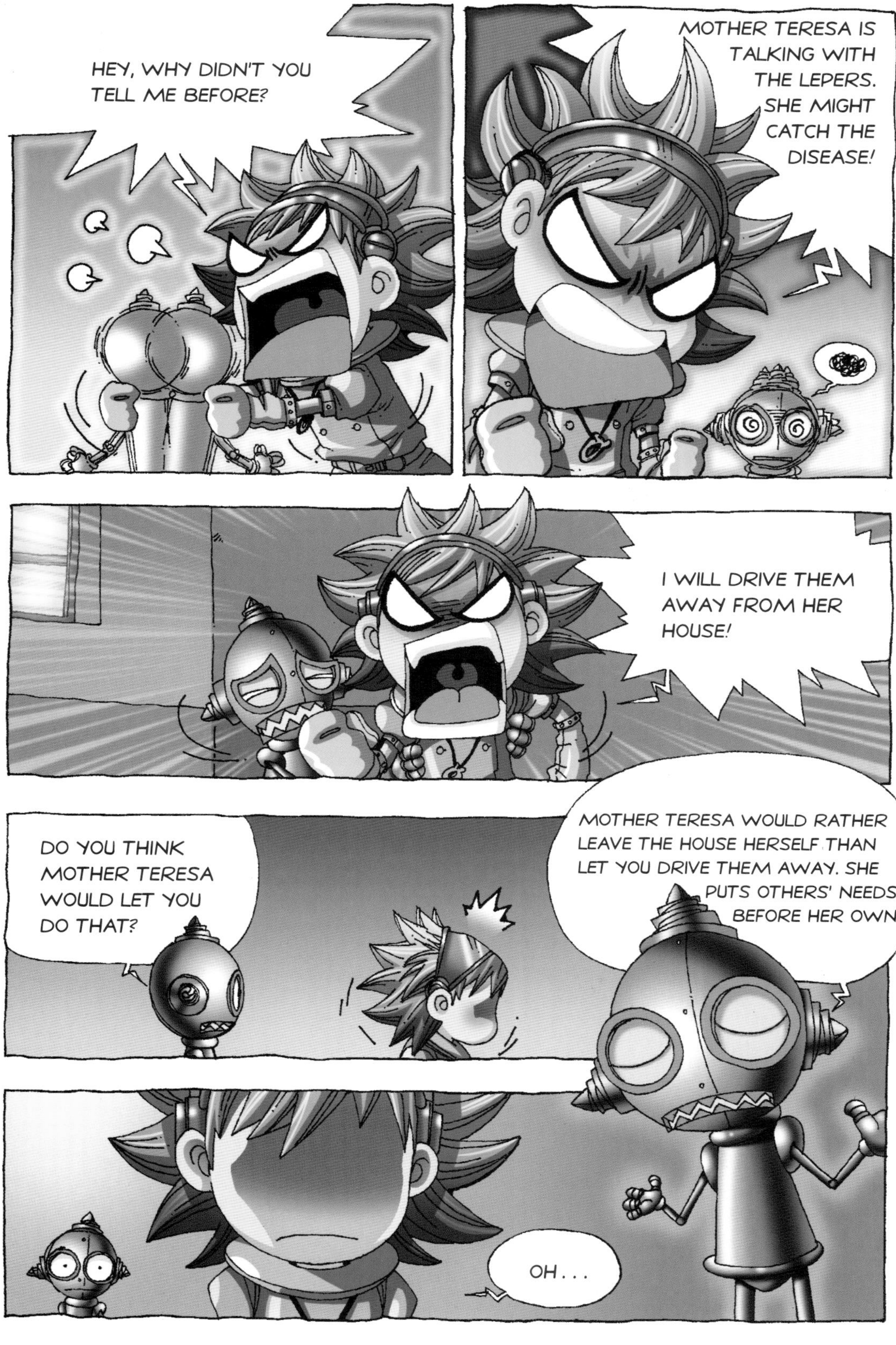
HEY, WHY DIDN'T YOU TELL ME BEFORE?
MOTHER TERESA IS TALKING WITH THE LEPERS. SHE MIGHT CATCH THE DISEASE!
I WILL DRIVE THEM AWAY FROM HER HOUSE!
DO YOU THINK MOTHER TERESA WOULD LET YOU DO THAT?
MOTHER TERESA WOULD RATHER LEAVE THE HOUSE HERSELF THAN LET YOU DRIVE THEM AWAY. SHE PUTS OTHERS' NEEDS BEFORE HER OWN.
OH . . .

MOTHER TERESA WILL HANDLE THIS. WHY DON'T WE JUST WATCH.

BUT . . . BUT . . .

WHERE ARE YOU TRAVELING TO?

WE WERE FORCED TO LEAVE OUR HOMES BECAUSE WE ARE LEPERS. SO WE ARE GOING TO TATANAGAR, WHERE THERE IS A LEPER'S VILLAGE.

BUT I DON'T WANT TO GO.

WE HAVE HEARD THAT TATANAGAR IS A PLACE OF DEATH. IT DOES NOT HAVE ENOUGH MEDICINE OR ENOUGH FOOD. WE WILL SUFFER AND NO ONE WILL HELP US.

GOD SENT THEM TO ME BECAUSE HE WANTS ME TO HELP THEM.

DEAR LORD...I WILL HELP YOUR PEOPLE, NO MATTER WHAT.

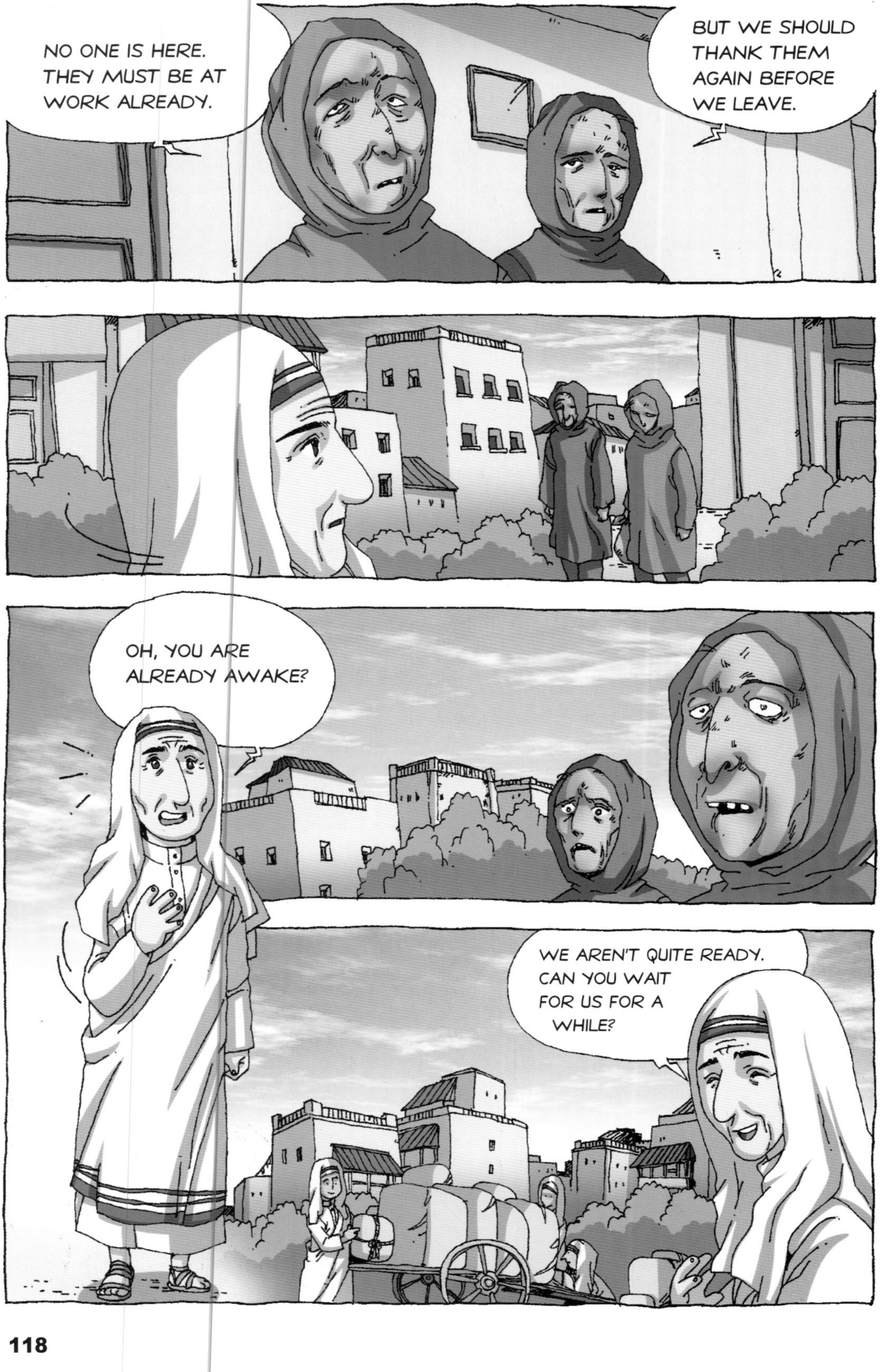
NO ONE IS HERE. THEY MUST BE AT WORK ALREADY.
BUT WE SHOULD THANK THEM AGAIN BEFORE WE LEAVE.
OH, YOU ARE ALREADY AWAKE?
WE AREN'T QUITE READY. CAN YOU WAIT FOR US FOR A WHILE?

WHAT? YOU AREN'T READY FOR WHAT?

WELL....

WE ARE COMING WITH YOU TO HELP THE LEPERS.

NO!

YOU MUST NOT COME WITH US.

LEPROSY IS CONTAGIOUS AND INCURABLE. WE APPRECIATE ALL YOUR KINDNESS, BUT . . .

ALL OF YOU WILL BECOME LEPERS YOURSELVES IF YOU GO THERE.

SOB SOB

119

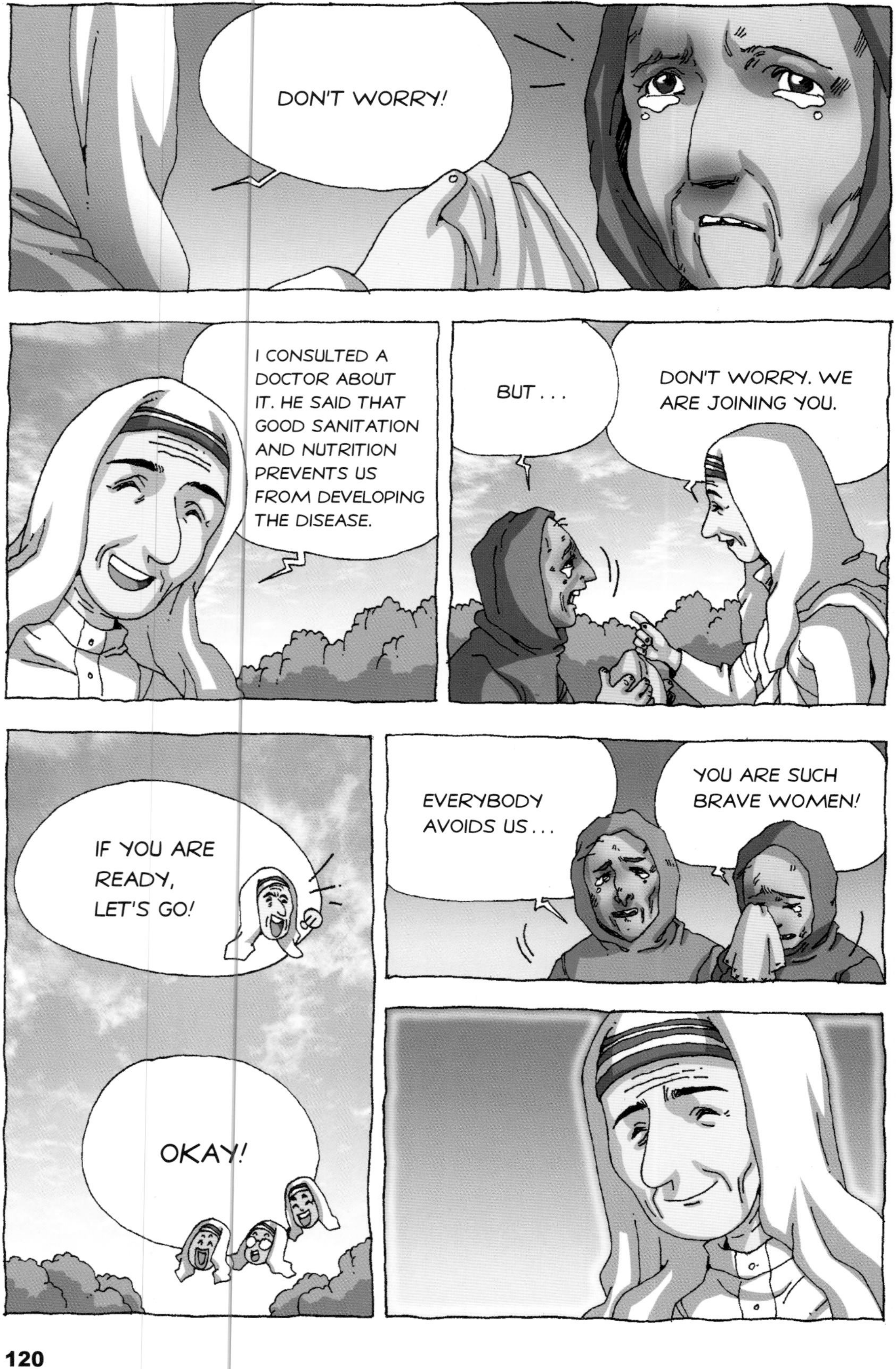
DON'T WORRY!
I CONSULTED A DOCTOR ABOUT IT. HE SAID THAT GOOD SANITATION AND NUTRITION PREVENTS US FROM DEVELOPING THE DISEASE.
BUT . . .
DON'T WORRY. WE ARE JOINING YOU.
IF YOU ARE READY, LET'S GO!
OKAY!
EVERYBODY AVOIDS US . . .
YOU ARE SUCH BRAVE WOMEN!

Lepers' Village In Tatanagar

HOW CAN PEOPLE LIVE IN THIS BARREN LAND? THIS IS MISERABLE.

AT THAT TIME, THEY MISTAKENLY THOUGHT THAT LEPROSY COULD BE TRANSMITTED THROUGH PHYSICAL CONTACT WITH LEPROUS PATIENTS. PEOPLE WHO HAD LEPROSY WERE FORCED TO LIVE IN COMMUNITIES WITH OTHER LEPERS, AWAY FROM CITIES.

IT'S TERRIBLE.

DON'T MAKE FACES.

THEY CARRY BIG WOUNDS IN THEIR HEARTS BECAUSE THEY HAVE BEEN SHUNNED BY THEIR FAMILIES AND NEIGHBORS. THEY WILL NOT TRUST US IF WE ACT SCARED OR DISGUSTED.

I'M SO SORRY!

WELL, SMILE EVERYONE!

YES, MOTHER TERESA!

122

In September 1957, Mother Teresa arrived in the leper village. She and the nuns started working to help the ill, despite the bad conditions of the patients and the village.

Mother Teresa opened a free medical center to help treat patients' specific symptoms.

Free Medical Center

At first, the lepers did not know what to think of this new group of energetic women. But soon they were impressed by the women's dedication and fearlessness.

THANK YOU FOR TREATING US SO WELL. OTHERS ACT AS THOUGH WE ARE NOT HUMAN.

BUT ALL OF YOU ARE VALUABLE CHILDREN OF GOD.

Thanks to the hard work of Mother Teresa and other volunteers, the village in Tatanagar became a better place to live.

However, they soon faced another problem.

A huge group of lepers traveled to the village when they heard what the women were doing there.

OUR MEDICAL CENTER IS TOO SMALL AND CROWDED WITH PATIENTS. WHAT CAN WE DO?

HMM . . .

I THINK WE HAVE TO EXPAND THE VILLAGE FOR THE PATIENTS.

THAT IS A GOOD IDEA. BUT WE NEED A LOT OF MONEY TO BUILD ANYTHING NEW.

I HAVE AN IDEA. WE CAN HAVE A FUNDRAISING CAMPAIGN TO COLLECT DONATIONS.

Mother Teresa held media interviews to ask for donations. She had become well known for her work with the sick and the orphans.

Medical Center

LEPROSY IS NOT AN INCURABLE DISEASE. BUT THEY NEED TREATMENT.

WITH BETTER TREATMENT, THESE PEOPLE CAN HAVE STRONG BODIES AND MINDS JUST AS YOU DO.

FOR THAT, WE NEED A PLACE WHERE THESE PATIENTS CAN BE TREATED. UNFORTUNATELY, WE DON'T HAVE ENOUGH MONEY TO BUY LAND TO BUILD A BETTER MEDICAL CENTER.

WE NEED YOUR HELP. PLEASE SUPPORT OUR MISSION.

PLEASE HELP THE LEPROUS PATIENTS.

FATHER! FATHER!

I KNOW WHAT YOU ARE GOING TO SAY.

YOU CAN PUT THIS MONEY IN THE FUNDRAISER BOX.

YES, FATHER! IT IS GOOD TO HELP OTHERS!

Many people collected donations across the nation. Even people from around the world sent money to her.

THANK YOU FOR YOUR COOPERATION.

The highest authority of the Catholic Church, the pope, also joined the campaign.

When Pope Paul VI visited India in 1964, he donated his luxury car for the cause. Mother Teresa sold the car to help pay for the village.

With the donated money and government support, Mother Teresa bought land 200 miles from Calcutta.

There, they constructed a village that was big enough to accept all the lepers of Calcutta.

During of the village the construction, volunteers workers worked with the lepers.

IT'S REALLY GOOD TO SEE THE LEPERS WORKING SIDE BY SIDE WITH ORDINARY PEOPLE.

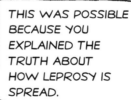

THIS WAS POSSIBLE BECAUSE YOU EXPLAINED THE TRUTH ABOUT HOW LEPROSY IS SPREAD.

NO. THIS IS THE RESULTS OF GOD'S LOVE FILLING EVERYONE'S HEARTS.

After 5 years, in 1968, the village of Shanti Nagar was completed.

Mother Teresa named the village Shanti Nagar, the "City of Peace."

The City of Peace had everything it needed: houses, places to work, places to sleep, hospitals, and even a nursery.

As the City of Peace was established, Mother Teresa helped the patients to take care of themselves.

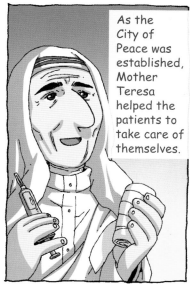

She taught them basic medical treatment to help ease their sufferings.

She also held job training for the leprous patients, so that when they healed and returned home, they would be able to make a living.

PUSH, PUSH!

CONGRATULATIONS. IT'S A BOY. HE IS HEALTHY AND BEAUTIFUL.

I CAN'T BELIEVE I GAVE BIRTH TO A HEALTHY BOY...

Mother Teresa transformed the leper colony from a city of death to a city of life.

I FEEL LIKE I'M DREAMING!

EPISODE 8
MOTHER TERESA GOES HOME TO GOD

After building the City of Peace, Mother Teresa expanded the Missionaries of Charity to help even more people.

In 1965, a Missionaries of Charity order was created in Venezuela, the first of hundreds outside of India.

In 1963, the Missionaries of Charity Brothers was created to help men get involved with Mother Teresa's missionary activities.

The Brothers orders were established in many regions of India, including Calcutta.

More and more volunteer workers came from all over the world to help Mother Teresa in her endless work.

I HAVE TRAVELED FROM SPAIN. I AM A NURSE.

WELCOME! PLEASE GO TO THE WOMAN OVER THERE. SHE WILL SHOW HOW YOU CAN HELP US.

THANK YOU!

WELCOME!

HAVE YOU COME HERE TO DO SOME VOLUNTEE WORK?

The volunteers were of different races and religions.

However, they had one thing in common. All of them were willing to help the poor and the sick without expecting rewards.

SOME WHO COULDN'T DO VOLUNTEER WORK COLLECTED GENEROUS CHARITY DONATIONS, IN ORDER TO SUPPORT THE ACTIVITIES BY CREATING A SUPPORTING ORGANIZATION.

IT HAD MORE THAN 40,000 MEMBERS IN THE WORLD, INCLUDING 14,000 FROM ENGLAND AND 6,000 FROM THE U.S. PEOPLE FROM FRANCE, BELGIUM, AUSTRIA, SPAIN, AND ITALY ALSO JOINED THE ORGANIZATION.

THANKS TO THE SUPPORT OF SO MANY PEOPLE, THE MISSIONARIES OF CHARITY COULD HELP THE POOR IN AFRICAN NATIONS SUCH AS TANZANIA AND ETHIOPIA.

HURRAY FOR THE MISSIONARIES OF CHARITY!

As the Missionaries of Charity grew. Mother Teresa became busier.

She went every place in India and in the world where she was needed.

She even took the risk of getting killed in a war at the age of 72.

BANG

She rescued the disabled children who had been trapped in an orphanage in West Beirut, where Israel and Arab countries were fighting.

In 1976, she went on to Guatemala to help the victims of a big earthquake.

Her love and service were known to the world. Mother Teresa was awarded the Pope John XXIII Peace Prize in 1971.

In December 1979, she received the Nobel Peace Prize.

THE NOBEL PEACE PRIZE IS ONE OF THE MOST IMPORTANT AWARDS IN THE WORLD. IT IS GIVEN TO THOSE WHO DEDICATE THEIR LIVES TO BUILDING WORLD PEACE.

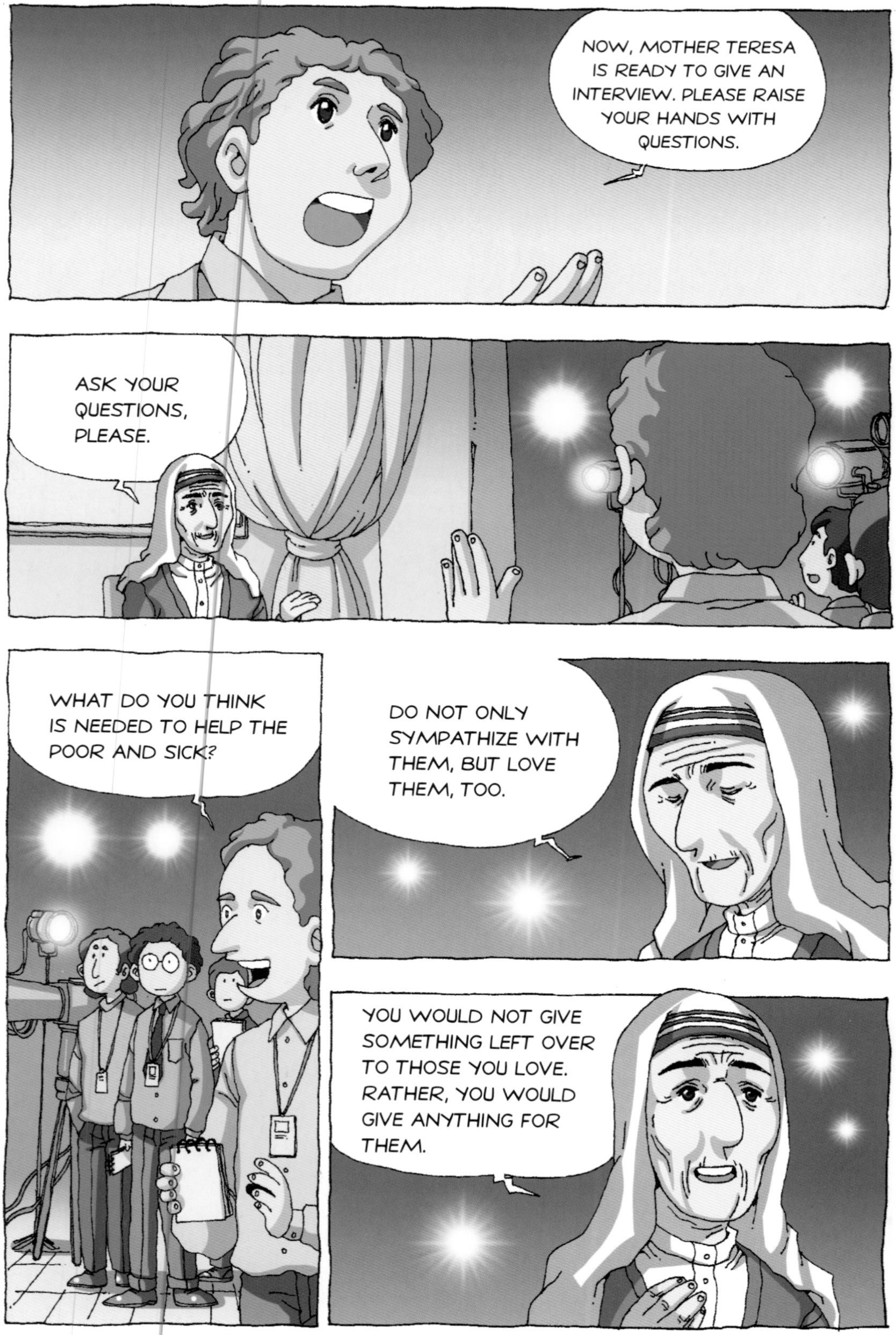
NOW, MOTHER TERESA IS READY TO GIVE AN INTERVIEW. PLEASE RAISE YOUR HANDS WITH QUESTIONS.
ASK YOUR QUESTIONS, PLEASE.
WHAT DO YOU THINK IS NEEDED TO HELP THE POOR AND SICK?
DO NOT ONLY SYMPATHIZE WITH THEM, BUT LOVE THEM, TOO.
YOU WOULD NOT GIVE SOMETHING LEFT OVER TO THOSE YOU LOVE. RATHER, YOU WOULD GIVE ANYTHING FOR THEM.

LOVE AND RESPECT THEM LIKE YOUR FAMILY. THAT IS HOW WE WILL BUILD A PEACEFUL WORLD.

PLEASE REMEMBER, LITTLE THINGS ARE INDEED LITTLE, BUT TO BE FAITHFUL IN LITTLE THINGS IS A GREAT THING.

WOW, SHE IS VERY INSPIRING!

Mother Teresa's work wasn't limited to the poor nations.

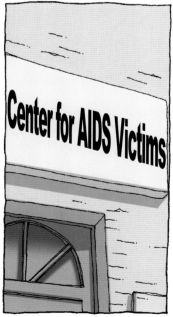

Center for AIDS Victims

In 1985, Mother Teresa launched the first center for AIDS victims in New York City. She took care of them just as she had helped those who suffered from leprosy.

She traveled all over the world to help those who need her and worked energetically despite her age and failing health.

But Mother Teresa, like all of us, had a limited lifetime.

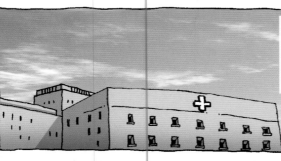

On September 5, 1997, Mother Teresa finished her morning prayer, went to Mass, spoke to the poor and abandoned, returned her room, and wrote thank you notes as she usually did.

She was planning to go church for the sacrament at 4 in the afternoon but she couldn't get up because her back hurt too much. After finishing her evening prayer, she silently talked with God.

SISTER, I CAN'T BREATHE.

OH NO, MOTHER! LET ME HELP YOU!

Mother, open your eyes, please.

WHAT IS WRONG WITH HER?

UNFORTUNATELY, SHE IS OLD AND ILL.

MOTHER TERESA HAS BEEN HOSPITALIZED BEFORE.

SHE HAD SUFFERED PROBLEMS WITH HER ARTERIES, AND IN 1990 SHE HAD A HEART ATTACK.

BUT SHE WORKED HARD AFTER THAT. DID SHE CONTINUE TO WORK FOR OTHERS EVEN THOUGH SHE WAS SICK?

THAT'S RIGHT. AFTER HER HEART ATTACK, SHE TRIED TO GIVE UP HER POSITION AS LEADER OF THE MISSIONARIES OF CHARITY, BUT EVERYONE VOTED FOR HER ANYWAY. SHE WAS SUCH A STRONG, ENERGETIC LEADER.

MOTHER TERESA REALLY LOVES AND CARES MORE ABOUT OTHERS THAN ABOUT HERSELF.

MOTHER TERESA, I WISH YOU COULD LIVE FOREVER.

SOB SOB

Mother Teresa knew that it was time for her to return to God. She held out her hand, touched the cross, and kissed it for the last time.

MY DEAR CHILD, TERESA.

OH, FATHER . . .

Mother Teresa surrendered her spirit to God that day in 1997, at the age of 87.

Everyone in the world, religious and nonreligious, paid tribute to Mother Teresa. India held a national funeral, the first since Mahatma Gandhi had died in 1948.

OUR ANGEL HAS RETURNED TO GOD.

SHE HAS LEFT US. NOW WE ARE ALL LIKE ORPHANS . . .

Her funeral was attended by hundreds of people from various religions and cultures. The thousands of people she had helped mourned her death.

MOTHER TERESA SHOWED GREAT LOVE. SHE WASHED THE WOUNDS OF DYING PEOPLE AND RELIEVED THEIR PAIN.

Cardinal Angelo Sodano

After the funeral, her body was taken to the headquarters of the Missionaries of Charity.

1.5 million people walked the streets to the center and said farewell to her, throwing flowers.

Mother Teresa had begun her voluntary work when she was 38. For 50 years, she had loved and taken care of the people that no one else wanted to take care of. She showed people how to be as caring and compassionate as Christ.

THE MISSIONARIES OF CHARITY, FOUNDED BY MOTHER TERESA, HAS 4,000 MEMBERS IN 120 COUNTRIES. THEY PUT HER LOVE INTO ACTION BY OPERATING HUNDREDS OF ORPHANAGES, MEDICAL RELIEF CENTERS, HOSPICE CENTERS FOR AIDS PATIENTS, AND OTHER PHILANTHROPIC ORGANIZATIONS.

EPILOGUE

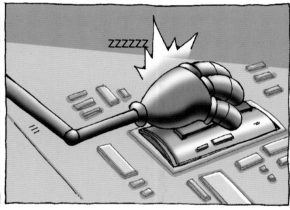

ZZZZZZ

MOTHER TERESA WAS A REALLY BEAUTIFUL PERSON. I CAN'T WAIT TO REFINE HER SPIRITUAL ENERGY.

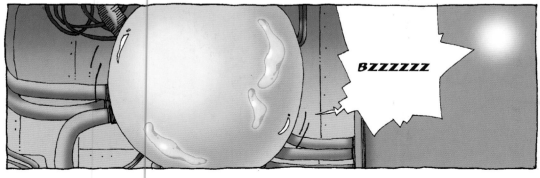

BZZZZZZ

OH, HERE IT COMES.

5, 4...

3, 2, 1.

DING!

COMPASSION!

COMPASSION!

THERE IT IS! THE COMPASSION FAIRY!

Name: Compassion Fairy. When dusted with powder from this fairy, you will make sacrifices for others and love them as you love yourself.

I WANT TO USE IT FIRST!

!

HMM, I WONDER IF IT WILL WORK. HE'S PRETTY SELFISH.

ALPHA PLUS, YOU LOOK TIRED. WHAT CAN I DO FOR YOU?

HUH?

THE COMPASSION FAIRY CAN MAKE EVEN SING KIND AND GENEROUS! NOW OUR MISSIONS WILL BE A LOT MORE FUN!

CAN I CLEAN YOUR ROOM? WOULD YOU LIKE SOMETHING TO DRINK? I WILL WRITE ALL OF THE REPORTS SO THAT YOU CAN REST!

WHY IS MOTHER TERESA IMPORTANT?

❖ Mother Teresa was honored with many awards throughout her life that recognized her tireless efforts. Her honors include the Pope John XXIII Peace Prize, the Nehru Award, the Balzan Prize, the Templeton Award, the 1979 Nobel Peace Prize, and many others.

❖ In 1982 Mother Teresa helped negotiate a ceasefire in Beirut between Palestinians and Israelis in order to rescue thirty-seven children trapped in a hospital.

❖ Mother Teresa was one of the first people to set up homes for AIDS victims. In 1985 she opened the Gift of Love house in New York to assist AIDS patients.

❖ In just over 45 years, Mother Teresa's Missionaries of Charity has been established in 130 countries, cared for 7,000 children, and treated over 3 million others.

❖ The Mother Teresa Award was created by the St. Bernadette Institute of Sacred Art in New Mexico to "recognize the achievements of those who beautify the world." Some past recipients of the award are President Jimmy Carter, Pope John Paul II, Dr. Maya Angelou, Nelson Mandela, and Archbishop Desmond Tutu of South Africa.

❖ Leprosy, a bacterial infection of the skin, was extremely common when Mother Teresa lived in India, yet there was little help available for lepers. To help leprosy victims, Mother Teresa and her Sisters took medicine and mobile health units directly onto the streets and into leper colonies.

❖ Two years after her death, Mother Teresa was named one of Time Magazine's 100 Most Important People of the Century in the Heroes and Icons category.

MOTHER TERESA'S WORLD

When	What
1910s–20s	**1910** Agnes Gonxha Bojaxhiu, later known as Mother Teresa, is born **1912** The *Titanic* sinks, killing 1513 people **1913** Albert Schweitzer opens a hospital in the French Congo **1914–1919** World War I **1920** Women in the United States are finally granted the right to vote **1929** The U.S. stock market crash leads to the Great Depression
1930s	**1930** Pluto is discovered **1932** Mahatma Gandhi protests India's class system by fasting **1933** Hitler becomes the leader of Germany **1939** World War II begins
1940s	**1942** Mahatma Gandhi starts the Quit India campaign to convince Britain to make India independent **1942–43** Famine kills as many as two million people in India **1945** World War II ends **1947** India gains its independence from Britain **1948** The World Health Organization is founded **1948** Mahatma Gandhi is assassinated in India
1950s	**1950** Mother Teresa founds her own order, the Missionaries of Charity **1953** Hilary and Norgay are the first men to reach the summit of Mt. Everest **1955** Salk invents the polio vaccine **1957** The Civil Rights Act is passed in the United States **1959** Tibet's spiritual leader, the Dalai Lama, flees to India when China crushes the Tibetan rebellion

	What
1960s	**1963** Martin Luther King, Jr, gives his "I have a dream" speech **1965** India and Pakistan are at war **1966** Indira Gandhi is elected Prime Minister of India **1969** Neil Armstrong is the first man to walk on the moon
1970s	**1972** Mother Teresa is awarded the Nehru Prize for her work in promoting peace and understanding throughout the world **1973** New York's World Trade Center Towers are built **1974** A smallpox epidemic in India kills almost 20,000 people **1974** India successfully conducts its first nuclear test **1978** The world's first "test tube baby" is born **1979** Mother Teresa is awarded the Nobel Peace Prize
1980s	**1981** The AIDS epidemic is first recognized **1981** The first U.S. space shuttle is launched **1984** Under Indira Gandhi's direction, troops storm the Golden Temple, killing more than 1,000 people **1984** A deadly gas leak in Bhopal, India, causes many deaths and injuries
1990s	**1992** The Internet Society is formed, marking the beginning of global web surfing **1992** Hindu–Muslim riots erupt in India **1995** The Murrah Federal Building in Oklahoma City is bombed **1997** Princess Diana is killed in an automobile accident **1997** Mother Teresa dies

On the Web

MOTHER TERESA OF CALCUTTA CENTER
www.motherteresa.org/layout.html

This extensive, interactive biographical site contains photographs, videos, paintings, Powerpoint presentations, and more, all related to Mother Teresa and her life. Click on "Creative Presentations" and then "Puzzles" to put together some jigsaw puzzles of Mother Teresa photographs.

"A DAY IN THE LIFE," TIME FOR KIDS
www.timeforkids.com/TFK/teachers/aw/ns/article/0,28138,610670,00.html

Find out what it's like to live as an eleven year old in India. This website also offers background information about India, a page where you can learn some Indian words and phrases, and a short quiz to test yourself about all you've discovered.

"MOTHER TERESA: ANGEL OF MERCY," CNN
www.cnn.com/WORLD/9709/mother.teresa/index.html

Learn more about Mother Teresa's life and death at this site. Videos, audio clips, slideshows, and quotes from Mother Teresa are included throughout.

UNITED STATES FUND FOR UNICEF
www.unicefusa.org/site/pp.asp?c=hkIXLdMRJtE&b=1706915

Would you like to learn more about how you can help poor and homeless children? Visit this site to see how you can make a difference along with the United Nations Children's Fund. And while you're there, try your hand at the UNICEF World Heroes game.

At the Library

MOTHER TERESA
by Demi (Margeret K. McElderry Books, 2005)

This award-winning picture book includes detailed information about Mother Teresa's life and will appeal to all ages. Author/illustrator Demi's fabulous artwork, with its unique, shimmering gold accents, makes this book stunningly beautiful.

MOTHER TERESA
by Haydn Middleton (Heinemann Library, 2001)

This photo-illustrated biography outlines Mother Teresa's life from birth to death. It includes several sidebars throughout that include quotes from Mother Teresa and others. Also included is a brief timeline of Mother Teresa's life, a glossary of terms, and a short list of other books about Mother Teresa.

AMELIA TO ZORA: TWENTY-SIX WOMEN WHO CHANGED THE WORLD
by Cynthia Chin-Lee (Charlesbridge, 2005)

Learn about other women who have made a major impact on our world. This illustrated book includes twenty-six short biographies of some very important women—Amelia Earhart, Helen Keller, Jane Goodall, Kristi Yamaguchi, Mother Teresa, and many others.

GREAT PEOPLE OF THE 20TH CENTURY
by the editors of Time Magazine (Time-Life Books, 1998)

You won't want to miss these stories about the people—from Charlie Chaplin to Martin Luther King, Jr. and Mother Teresa—who shaped the 20th century. Their stories will show you the many different ways that people can improve our world.

The Saint of the Gutters Gives All

Because Mother Teresa was well-known throughout the world, it might be easy to believe that she lived the life of a celebrity, but nothing could be further from the truth. Mother Teresa sacrificed every comfort in order to identify with the "poorest of the poor."

She owned only three saris (the traditional dress of Indian women), and when someone offered to donate a washing machine to the order, Mother Teresa refused it. She and the Sisters washed their clothes in metal buckets instead.

Once Pope Paul VI gave Mother Teresa an expensive gift—a fancy car. Do you think she kept it? No! As the story goes, she never even drove it. She immediately auctioned it off and used the money to help build a leper colony.

In 1979, when Mother Teresa won the Nobel Peace Prize, she asked organizers to forego the traditional banquet and instead use the banquet money to buy food for the poor of Calcutta. Mother Teresa was a remarkable woman who did not hesitate to give up her own personal comfort for the needs of others.